THE WITCH'S LADDER

WITCHES OF PALMETTO POINT SERIES

WENDY WANG

CHAPTER 1

The metal shopping buggy rattled and shook on the uneven asphalt of the Piggly Wiggly parking lot on the south end of Palmetto Point. Charlie Payne pulled her keys from her purse and put her finger on the unlock button to unload her groceries. As a psychic, she hated coming here, because being the only grocery store in a town this size meant that no matter when she came there was always a crowd. Her chance encounters with people and the ghosts still attached to them went up exponentially and it only got worse the closer they got to the summer when tourists would flood the town and the nearby beaches. The tourists could always drive the forty minutes up Highway 17 to West Ashley, one of the suburbs of Charleston, South Carolina. But if they didn't stop to get their groceries on the way to the beach, The Pig, as it was known locally, was the best and only choice once they arrived in Palmetto Point.

Her last visit to the store was over two weeks ago when she had accidentally brushed against a man, and the apparition of his screaming dead mother appeared. The woman followed Charlie around the store nagging her to tell him what an idiot he was for giving that woman he married her engagement ring because the man's new bride had taken the ring and sold the diamond. After pocketing the cash she replaced the stone with cubic zirconia. Charlie's head had begun to pound by the time she made it to the dairy section and when she could take it no more, she turned to the woman and told her there was no way she was going to ruin the man's new marriage because of a ghost with a grudge. She abandoned her buggy in the middle of the store, ignoring the stares of the people around her. For the next two weeks she ended up eating at her cousin Jen's restaurant, The Kitchen Witch Café, for almost every meal.

Thankfully not one person had touched her today but as she approached the row and parked her car, the hair on the back of her neck pricked up and she glanced around looking for the culprit. The afternoon sky had clouded over when she arrived at The Pig and was darker now. Thunder rumbled in the distance. She slowed down to watch a man peering into the windows of the car next to hers. He cursed under his breath and moved on to her car.

He was tall and brawny and wore faded jeans, work boots, and a T-shirt with the arms cut out. He had two tattoos on his left arm. A skull with a snake threading through one eye socket on his upper arm and a snake coiled around the handle of a dagger on his left forearm. He started to bend over and peer inside her blue Honda Civic. He shielded his eyes from the sun with his hands.

Charlie looked around the parking lot to see if anyone else was nearby. A mother was wrangling her two-year-old into her minivan and some teenagers were hanging around the back of a pickup truck a row over. A man and his teenage son walked past her. If she got in trouble, she could scream and hopefully somebody would at least turn their heads.

"Excuse me?" Charlie said using a firm voice she reserved mainly for her eleven-year-old son. "Is there something I can help you with?"

The man stopped mid-bend and stood up straight. He looked her up and down in a way that made her feel naked. "I'm sure I could think of something."

"That's my car," she said in a tone that clearly meant she was not having it. "Would you like to explain why you're looking in *my* car?"

He chuckled but there was something condescending about it that made her bristle. "Well, if you must know my stepdaughter snuck out to be with her friends. I saw her take off across the parking lot toward these cars. I'm just checking to make sure she's not hiding in somebody's backseat."

"Well, my car is locked so ..." she said.

His lips twisted into a smirk. Charlie pulled her phone from her purse.

"Now I need to get in my car," she said.

The man held his arms up in surrender to step backwards away from her car. "Go right ahead."

She popped the trunk with her key and watched him cautiously as she loaded her groceries into the trunk of her car.

When she finally got into the driver seat, she immediately locked the doors and watched him from her rearview mirror. After a few minutes he stood in the middle of the parking lot lane and screamed, "Ryan Whisnant you better pray I don't find you here!" He stalked off and got into a big black pickup truck with silver flames painted on the side.

Charlie rolled her eyes. She put her key in the ignition and turned the engine over.

"Wait," a small voice said from behind her seat.

Charlie quickly turned her head and found a teenage girl wedged between the seats. She had her arms wrapped around her knees and her face hidden in the crook of her elbow.

"It's okay," Charlie said using her most soothing mother voice. The one she used when Evan had a nightmare. "He's gone."

The girl lifted her head. Her wide brown eyes flitted from Charlie to the window and back.

"How did you get in here?" Charlie asked. "I was sure I locked the door."

"I tried all the handles, and yours was the only one that opened."

"Well, I guess I'll need to be more careful from now on, don't I?" Charlie said. "Do you want me to drive you home? Or maybe you'd rather go to a friend's house? Someplace safe. He's your stepfather, right?"

"Yeah, I just have to wait until he cools off. I don't know if you could tell or not but he was drunk."

"Is he like that often?" Charlie asked.

The girl looked away and lifted herself out of the cramped space, sitting on the edge of the back seat. "I don't live far from here. I can walk."

"You know I have a friend that can help you. I work with the police sometimes."

The girl's long thin face shifted from scared to terrified. "No. Please don't tell the police."

"Has he hurt you?"

The girl swallowed hard and shook her head before answering, "No."

Charlie immediately knew it was a lie, but she

also knew that things like this were complicated and not always easily solved with lots of questions. She reached into her purse and pulled out a black plastic card case, opened it and pulled out one of her cards.

"My name is Charlie Payne. This is my cell phone number." She pointed to the embossed telephone number on the front of her card. "I want you to call me if you're in trouble. Okay? And I'll come get you and we'll figure it out together okay?"

"Why would you help me?" The girl glanced down at the card, reading it carefully.

"I used to have a husband who could be loud and scary. I know what that feels like."

"Was he a drunk too?"

"No, he didn't drink. But he was very controlling. And he made my life hard."

"But you left him, right?"

"Yeah, I did. It was the hardest thing I ever had to do but I did it."

Ryan let out a sigh. "My mom will never leave my stepfather."

"How old are you?"

"Sixteen and a half. I'll be seventeen in September."

"When you turn eighteen, you become an adult. You can leave."

The girl nodded. "This says you're a psychic. Is that true?"

"Yes."

"You help the police?"

"Sometimes."

"Can you tell the future?"

"Sometimes. Sometimes I can tell the past and sometimes I can talk to spirits."

"You talk to ghosts?" The girl rubbed her thumb over the card.

"I do," Charlie said matter-of-factly. "A lot of times, people come to me to help them connect with a dead loved one or to figure out the direction of their life."

The girl turned the card over and saw the embossed pentacle on the back. "Is that a pentagram? Are you a devil worshipper?"

"No," Charlie chuckled. "Of course not. That's not a symbol of the devil. It's used by witches for protection. It's a good thing. Not evil."

"So, are you like, a witch?" The girl asked her tone full of curiosity.

Charlie took a deep breath and nodded. "I am."

"You can do spells and stuff?" The girl leaned forward, mesmerized by the conversation.

"I can, when it's needed," Charlie said.

"So ... are there any spells that could kill somebody?" Her voice lowered on the word kill.

Charlie frowned. She knew where this was going. "Yeah, there are, but they're forbidden."

"Forbidden by who?"

"By any witch that adheres to the principles of light," Charlie said. "A curse or killing spell is dark magic. It's destructive and causes an imbalance in the world. Witches who practice white magic seek balance. So we take an oath to harm no one."

The girl made a noise in her throat and seemed to be thinking over Charlie's explanation. She muttered softly to herself, "Do no harm."

"What's your name?"

"Ryan."

"I can't give you a curse Ryan, but I can give you a blessing. Would you like that?"

The girl tilted her head and a slight smile curved her lips. "A blessing. I like that."

Charlie reached around her neck and unfastened the silver necklace she always wore. "Here, put this on." Charlie gestured for the girl to lean forward further and she slipped it around the girl's neck. "This necklace was given to me to protect me. And I'm giving it to you to protect you. The pendant is a pentacle and the two gemstones are black tourmalines."

"Wow," the girl whispered touching the pendant.

Charlie placed her hand on the girl's shoulder and closed her eyes. Taking a deep breath, she focused her energy as she spoke. "Protect this child with light that is pure. Protect her day and night, from those who would do her harm. May this shield remain unbroken. So mote it be."

"That was amazing," the girl said softly, sounding a little drunk. "I totally felt that."

"Good. Keep hold of that feeling when you're scared."

Ryan smiled and nodded. "I will. Thank you. I really should go now."

"You sure I can't drop you off?" Charlie asked.

"Yeah, I'm sure."

"Okay, be careful out there."

"I will."

Charlie watched as Ryan got out of her car and walked back over to the teenagers standing around a truck. Ryan said something to one of the other girls then waved and started walking away toward the road that ran along The Piggly Wiggly to the housing development behind the large shopping center. Her hand drifted to the bare skin where her pendant used to hang and an uneasy feeling settled over her. She hoped the blessing would hold and that the girl would be all right.

* * *

CHARLIE HELD THE PAPER BAG WITH FOUR MUFFINS IN one hand and a large fresh coffee in the other as she approached the apartment of Deputy Jason Tate. She pressed the button for the doorbell with her index finger. Inside she could hear the loud ding dong ding dong. She put her ear to the door and waited. Then it occurred to her he might not be home. She knew he wasn't working but maybe ... maybe he wasn't home. Maybe he was spending the night with that social worker. Was he even still seeing her? Charlie took a step back away from the door. She should've called first. She turned and started down the hall heading for the staircase. Behind her the door opened.

"Charlie?" Jason said. He stepped out into the hallway wearing only a pair of khaki shorts. His short, sandy brown hair tousled as if he had just gotten out of bed. Charlie winced at her name and turned around.

"Hey—" she said her voice going up half an octave at the end. "I woke you up."

Jason rubbed his eyes and shook his head. "No, I've been up for a while. I just haven't gotten out of bed yet. What's going on?"

"I..." she held out the bag of muffins and coffee. "I brought you breakfast. I called the station and they said you weren't working today. I probably should've called first." Why was she talking so fast? She glanced away from his defined muscular chest, looking down at her feet.

"Thanks." He took the bag of muffins and the coffee. He glanced at the door and then at Charlie again. A soft redness filled his cheeks. "So why are you really here?"

Charlie sighed. "I had this strange experience yesterday and I wanted to talk to you about it."

"Now?"

"Yeah — if that's okay?"

His eyes darted back to the doorway again, and he pulled the door shut.

Charlie narrowed her eyes and gave him an accusatory grin. "You do have somebody here," she teased. "Anybody I know?"

Jason's eyes widened, and he cleared his throat and shook his head. "Uh ... no."

"No you're alone or no I don't know her?"

"No you don't know her."

Charlie cocked her head.

"You do know that I can tell when you're lying? Right?"

He frowned and sighed. "I'm not ready to share with you yet, how about that?"

Charlie snickered. "Fine," she said. "Maybe we can meet up later."

"Is somebody in trouble?"

"Maybe," Charlie said. "I don't know for sure."

"Where does this fall on a scale of 1 to 911?"

"It's not an emergency if that's what you're asking. At least I don't think it is. I had a stowaway in my car yesterday. A teenage girl hiding from her stepfather."

"Was she hurt?"

"Not that I could tell. She was just really scared." Charlie rocked on her feet.

"I don't know what I could do about that. It doesn't sound like a crime's been committed. Did you see any signs of abuse?"

"No. Not physical abuse anyway."

"Okay. So she didn't really make a complaint or anything then."

"Not exactly. But she said something to me ... and I had this dream last night. I'm just worried, that's all."

"What did she say?"

"I gave her my card and told her to call me if she needed help. She asked about the pentacle on the back of the card."

"So?"

"I told her what it meant and that I was a witch. She asked if I could do a curse."

"I'm not following you. She wanted you to curse somebody? Last time I checked cursing someone isn't a crime unless fraud is involved then maybe—"

"Jason," Charlie snapped. "You don't go to a shrink unless you want to be shrunk and you don't ask a witch for a curse unless you want to curse someone, which usually entails pain, suffering or death."

"Okay. What is it you want me to do exactly?"

"I don't know ... I guess I just wanted to talk to you about it."

Jason's face softened. "Why? You didn't give her a curse, right?"

"No, of course not."

Charlie looked around the apartment complex, gathering her thoughts. She knew Jason wanted to get back to his "friend," but she wasn't ready to leave. "Sometimes talking to you helps me make sense of things. You told me it's not a crime ... so ... I'm sorry I bothered you."

"Charlie," he sighed. "You're not bothering me, and I do appreciate the breakfast I really do. I—"

"I know. I can't stop thinking about her." Charlie said stepping forward, feeling a little desperate. "I think something bad is going happen to her but I can't stop that from happening."

Jason's face softened. "You don't even know this girl. Why do you care so much?"

"Because I'm a human being? Does there have to be a reason to care? I just do," she snapped.

"All right." Jason held his paper bag and coffee up in surrender. "I didn't mean to get your dander up. I—" he cleared his throat. "Why don't I meet you later today and we can talk about it more."

"No. It's fine. I'm fine. You and your company enjoy the muffins. I'll talk to you later."

"Why don't I meet you for lunch at the café?" He took a step closing the gap between them. "I really do want to hear about it."

"You're sweet." Charlie shrugged. "But that won't be necessary." She brushed her hand across his forearm. An image popped into her head of a woman with strawberry blond hair sitting up in his bed with the sheet wrapped around her naked body. A worry frown etched a deep line in her freckled, make-up free forehead, a line Charlie was very familiar with. Charlie's eyes widened, and her jaw slackened. Lisa, her cousin, was the woman.

"You okay?" Jason asked, concern washing over his handsome features.

Charlie cleared her throat, shaking it off. She forced a smile. "Yeah, I'm fine."

Jason's eyes tightened. "You sure?"

"Oh yeah, I'm good." Charlie glanced down at the watch on her left arm. "I should go."

"Okay." He took a sip of his coffee and closed his eyes with pleasure at the taste. "Perfect. I don't know how Jen does it, but this is always the best coffee."

"Yep. Just perfect." Charlie nodded and took a step back.

"I'll text you later, okay?"

"Sure. Later."

Charlie turned quickly and headed down the stairs, stomping on every step until she reached the bottom. She got into her car, put the key into the ignition and turned it. The engine roared to life. One hand gripped the steering wheel while the other gripped the gearshift so tightly her knuckles whitened. Her mind raced with questions. What the hell was Lisa doing with Jason? Charlie knew that Lisa and her boyfriend had broken up in February, but Jason? Jason was ... was what? Her partner? Her friend? None of those things changed if Lisa and Jason dated. Although when Lisa chewed up his heart and spit it out like a gristly piece of meat, it would certainly make inviting him to Friday night dinner awkward. She took a deep breath. Maybe she was wrong. Maybe she was imagining things. Maybe ...

Charlie glanced up at his building again. Nope. She could feel her cousin's presence now that she was aware of it and there was no mistaking it. She scowled, put the car into reverse and headed home, unsure what she should do with this new information.

CHAPTER 2

On Tuesday morning, Charlie scraped the wooden spoon through the eggs in the hot pan, stirring them into large lumps, just the way her eleven-year-old son Evan liked them. She glanced down at the flame, making sure it was at a near-simmer so as not to cook them too fast. Evan could be picky when it came to his eggs. One hint that they were brown, and her boy would wriggle his nose and draw his mouth into a frown and refuse to eat them. She needed to get him to school, run to the pharmacy to pick up a prescription and be at work by nine this morning. Too much to do for Evan to turn up his nose at her cooking today.

The television droned in the background as she scooped eggs onto a plate. A piece of toast popped up from the toaster and she laid it over the mound of yellow curds to keep them warm.

"Evan," she called, placing his plate on the bistro table against the far wall of the small kitchen. "Come on, honey. We're gonna be late. Get a move on."

She placed the pan in the bottom of the sink and rinsed the ancient cast-iron before giving it a good scrub with a dish brush. Something red caught her eye and she glanced out the window in front of her.

A large expanse of lush green grass separated her little cottage from the main house where her uncle and his daughter Jen and granddaughter Ruby lived. A pale layer of mist hovered just above the lawn, which had been manicured to within an inch of its life. Charlie saw her young cousin Ruby descending the back steps, a large white basket in one hand and bright red rubber boots on her feet. At first Ruby swung the basket as she walked and talked to herself. Charlie couldn't help but smile. The petite girl wore her long dark hair in a braid down her back. She stopped on the lawn and suddenly spun around, whipping her braid as she went.

Charlie chuckled and smiled wider. She loved that even at six Ruby wasn't afraid of walking, or in this case spinning, to her own drummer. She shook her head and shifted her attention back to her pan. She dried it with one of the red and white dish towels hanging on the hook by the sink, then put the pan back on the apartment-size stove to heat for a quick seasoning with bacon grease. She scooped a teaspoon of the nearly solid drippings into the center of the old pan and the slight scent of bacon filled the air as soon as it started to melt.

"Hey look, Mom," Evan said. His chair scraped across the tile floor and he took a seat. "That's the place we're supposed to go for our field trip next week."

Charlie looked up at the television. A pretty brunette reporter was talking about a body that had been found at the Seward Nature Preserve. Behind the reporter Charlie saw men in khaki and brown uniforms milling around the crime scene. She turned and folded her arms across her chest.

"I wonder if it's anybody we know," Evan said, sounding a little too excited. He broke his toast in half and began to butter it. Charlie frowned.

"Turn that off, sweetie. Come on and eat. We've got to get going."

Evan glanced at the stove. "Your pan is burning."

The heavy odor of acrid smoke hit her nostrils. "Dammit," she muttered. Quickly she turned off the burner, grabbed the hot pad hanging from a hook beside the stove and moved the smoking pan to a cool burner. With the twist of a knob the exhaust fan roared into action, but it wasn't enough to siphon away the billowing black cloud. Charlie unlocked the window over the sink and pushed up the sash.

Ruby stood frozen, her little body no longer spinning and dancing. Her red boots glistened with morning dew and the hair at the nape of Charlie's neck stood up. A second later a shrill little-girl scream echoed across the lawn, filling up the space between the houses.

"What was that?" Evan's fork clanked as he dropped it on the plate.

"It's Ruby. Stay here," Charlie warned. Another shriek, this one longer and more painful than the first, ruptured the quiet. Evan's blue eyes widened, and he hopped to his feet and was out the front door before she could stop him.

"Evan!" She followed him outside to scold him for not listening, but he was halfway across the yard headed toward the white clapboard chicken coop. The sight of her six-year-old cousin Ruby made her choke back the words. The child had fallen to her knees and her little body shook. Charlie broke into a run.

Evan skidded across the wet grass and knelt beside the little girl long before Charlie could get to them. He put his hand on her back and Ruby latched onto him, throwing her arms around his neck, almost knocking him over. Charlie came up behind them, her mind trying to make sense of what she was seeing. She touched her hand to Ruby's back, giving it a gentle pat.

"Holy shit," Charlie muttered under her breath. Bloodied mounds of white feathers lay scattered around the coop. "Oh my God," Charlie whispered as she walked among the bodies. A large metal bowl filled with chicken feed and table scraps lay on the ground, its contents untouched. Charlie felt her face go cold. The sound of Ruby weeping pulled her back and Charlie tried to keep her voice as steady as possible as she spoke.

"Evan carry her to the house and send Uncle Jack out."

"Yes ma'am." Evan glanced at the dead chickens and grimaced. He whispered something into Ruby's ear. She loosened her grip long enough for him to stand up. The normally sassy six-year-old sniffed back her tears as Evan picked her up. She wrapped her legs tightly around his mid-section and her arms around his neck. Her watery blue eyes stared at the chickens as they headed toward the tidewater-style house.

Charlie knelt next to one of the carcasses. Something about it just didn't seem right but she couldn't quite put her finger on what was wrong.

"What the hell happened?" Jack asked as he approached a few moments later. His red leathery face was a map of concern. "Evan said all the chickens were—" He stopped as soon as he saw the bodies. "Well shit."

"Good thing Jen's not here, or you'd owe the swear jar," Charlie said absently.

"Hell, Jen'll be able to put Ruby through college just from what she puts in that jar every week." He crossed his arms and surveyed the seven corpses.

Charlie poked at the body in front of her and it finally became apparent what was going on. She looked at the other bodies and recoiled. "Their heads are missing," she said her voice full of horror. "What would do this? A raccoon?"

Her uncle put a hand on her shoulder and dropped to one knee next to her. He grabbed the poor bird in front of them and flipped it over, examining it more closely.

"No animal I know could do this." He sounded angry and a little disgusted. "Look." He held up the bloody stump of one of the chicken's legs. "They took the feet. The only thing that would leave such a clean cut like this is a blade."

Her stomach churned. "Are you saying someone purposefully came onto the property and killed the chickens for their heads and feet?"

"Yep." Jack scrubbed his fingers through the bristly hair covering his chin and sighed. "I chased some teenagers off my dock a couple weeks ago. Could be their handiwork." His mouth disappeared into his wiry gray beard. "Son of a bitch. They were just getting to where they were laying good again."

She looked her uncle in the eye. "You should call the sheriff."

Jack shook his head. "Why? So he can take a report that's never gonna go anywhere?"

"It might," she countered, but she knew he was right.

"Nah. I'll just give them a proper burial and head over to the feed and seed."

Charlie nodded. "Well, I'm at least gonna let Jason know."

"All right you do that, and I'll see if Wilma Connors can get me some chicks as fast as she can."

Charlie sighed. "That'll help Ruby, I guess."

"Yeah, she loved these girls."

Near the edge of the woods between her uncle's property and the river, Charlie heard clucking sounds. Maybe one of the chickens had somehow escaped the others' fate. "You hear that?"

Jack's head tilted to one side, as if he were listening. The heavy lines on his forehead deepened. "I don't hear anything."

The clucking grew louder. "How can you not hear that? It's so loud. Hold on." Charlie rose to her feet and pulled her uncle up to standing. She headed toward the sound, her heart growing lighter. When she reached the edge of the tree line, she scanned the branches. Sitting on a low branch was a lone buff-colored chicken.

"We have a survivor!"

Jack stalked through the litter of chicken corpses toward her. "Where?"

"There." She pointed to the chicken sitting in the tree.

"I don't see anything." A quizzical expression deepened the lines of her uncle's face, making him look much older than his sixty-three years. "Where?"

"Right there." She continued to point. Charlie glanced from the chicken to her uncle and back again. She frowned with realization. The bird was just as dead as the others. "Well shit."

Her uncle gave her a smug look and held out his palm. "Guess I'm not the only one who owes the swear jar. Pay up."

Charlie shook her head and gave her uncle a don't-be-ridiculous look. "You first."

He smiled and scratched his head. "Can you drop Ruby off at school on your way out? Looks like I've got a mass grave to dig."

"You don't want to clean them and eat them?" Charlie half-teased.

"No way. One, because Ruby gave them all names. I don't really want to eat her pets, do you?"

Charlie wriggled up her nose. "Oh. No, definitely not."

"Secondly, do you have any idea what a pain in the ass it is to clean a chicken?"

Charlie shook her head. "Nope. Nor do I want to."

The spirit of the chicken continued to cluck over their heads. Charlie twisted her lips at the poor little thing. "You wouldn't happen to know the name of that buff colored chicken, would you?"

"That's Penny," he said. "Ruby's favorite."

"Of course it is," she muttered. How on earth was she supposed to help a dead chicken?

"Why?"

"No reason. I better get going or we're all be gonna be late."

* * *

THE LUNCH CROWD THINNED AT THE KITCHEN WITCH Cafe after two o'clock, giving Jen a chance to breathe before she had to pick up her daughter, Ruby, from school at 3:15. Her father had called her that morning and told her about the chickens. The thought of someone skulking around their hen house out of spite made her stomach turn over. She could keep spirits and other supernatural things off the property with carefully designed wards. People were trickier. She could sometimes turn them away but a lot of it depended on their will. If a person wanted to get on their property and was hell bent on doing it, there was very little white or even gray magic she knew of to completely stop it from happening.

Thankfully, her father had been there to deal with the chicken corpses because she didn't think she could have handled that today. What she could handle was Ruby's tender heart and her questions. That was Jen's specialty. She'd mulled over the antici- pated conversation all day, playing through different scenarios, different lines of questioning her preco- cious daughter might throw at her. She was prepared for anything her six-year-old might come up with.

After refilling the iced-tea for the couple sitting by the front window, she went through the cash drawer, counting it carefully, whittling it down to a hundred and fifty dollars of mostly twenties, tens, fives and ones. She slipped a rubber band around a stack of twenties and placed it inside the vinyl deposit pouch before she stuck it inside her green canvas messenger bag. She may as well make a bank run while she was out.

The bell jingled, and she looked up. Kristin Duguid walked in the door with a wide smile and a wave. Her fine blonde hair hung over her slim shoul- ders and her blue eyes glittered with light. Something that Jen hadn't seen in her friend's eyes in a long time.

"Well, hey Kristin," Jen said. "You're positively glowing. What's going on?"

"I can't talk about it yet."

"Well I know it's not a new job, since you own the pharmacy. So it must be a new man."

Kristin's fair cheeks colored a deep red and she giggled. "Jen stop. I'm not gonna talk about it right now."

"It is," Jen teased. "Kristin has a boyfriend."

"I promise you'll be the first to know when I have news," Kristin said, taking a seat at the counter. "Right now I just need to pick up the pie I ordered earlier. Is it ready?"

"Yes it is." Jen zipped up her messenger bag and shoved it into the cubby beneath the cash register. "I'll be right back." She disappeared into the kitchen and grabbed the plastic bag holding the chocolate pie with salted caramel drizzled on it.

"I haven't put forks and napkins in there yet," Evangeline said.

"I'll do it, don't worry," Jen said. "And then I've got to go get Ruby."

Jen made her way back to the counter and placed the plastic bag down in front of Kristin.

"Do you need eight forks or twelve?"

"Better make it eight, no twelve," Kristin said, shaking her head. "Just in case."

Jen counted out twelve plastic forks and grabbed

a stack of napkins and shoved it all into the plastic bag. Kristin pulled out her credit card and Jen rang up the transaction.

The bell jingled again and Jen looked up. A tall man she'd never seen before stood near the door, scanning the restaurant as if he were looking for someone. He was handsome in a baby-faced sort of way, with unruly brown hair that curled on his forehead. He was broad-shouldered and there was something mischievous in his blue eyes that charmed her, even from across the room. For a brief second their eyes met, and he flashed her a bright, white smile. It caught her off guard when her body reacted with a stomach flutter.

Kristin followed Jen's gaze and then gave her a sly smile. "Now who has a man?"

"Oh hush," Jen said handing Kristin her receipt. Kristin laughed and walked out making sure to say hello to the man as she passed him. He headed for the counter and took a seat, craning his neck at the expansive chalk-board menu that stretched the length of the back counter.

Jen called up her best customer-service smile, grabbed her order pad and pulled the pen from behind her ear.

"Hi," she said. "What can I get for you?"

"Well, what's good?" He folded his hands together.

28

"Everything," she said.

"Wow," he chuckled. "Is your boss close by or are you just that enthusiastic."

"Both," she grinned. "I *am* the boss, and yes, I am that enthusiastic."

"An enthusiastic entrepreneur and cute to boot. I guess it's my lucky day," he said.

Jen's cheeks filled with unexpected heat. Dealing with men flirting with her was a daily occurrence, and it ranged from subtle to sexual harassment. She'd removed her fair share of men's hands from her ass and once joked to Evangeline that she should put the skills needed to gently but firmly put a man in his place in the job description for new waitresses.

Maybe it was his smile or maybe it was the way his eyes glittered. Whatever it was it made her keenly aware of her attraction to him. Flirting back could mean making things easier for herself, a bigger tip or maybe even a return customer. She was fishing for none of those things, though, so she pretended to be more interested in her order pad than looking him in the eye. "I guess it is," she said. "So have you decided?"

"Uh — I think I'll try the grilled pimento cheese with homemade chips."

"Sounds good." She tested the waters and glanced at him. His smile had toned to a contented line, and she poured him a glass of water.

A few minutes later she served him and put the ticket down on the counter next to him.

"So, you're from here, I take it," he said, inspecting the oozing cheese sandwich. He brought it to his nose and sniffed it before taking his first bite.

"Born and raised." She smiled, loving to watch the faces of people when they tried her food for the first time. Even when she got a furrowed brow—as if the person wasn't sure exactly what they were tasting —there was almost always a little moan of pleasure.

His eyes rolled back in his head for a few seconds as the crunch of the buttery bread melded with the spicy cheese mix. "Mmm—my god, that's good," he said, covering his mouth with his hand. At least his mama had raised him right.

"Thanks," she chirped. "Glad you like it."

"Are you the chef here?" he asked.

"Chef, waitress, hostess, money-taker, bathroom scrubber." She chuckled to herself. "You name it. I do it."

"Very nice." He nodded, then wiped his hand on his pants and offered it to shake. "I'm Ben. Ben Sutton."

"Nice to meet you, Ben. Ben Sutton," she quipped, taking his hand. A chill raced up her arm leaving goose bumps in its wake. It had been a while since that had happened. Not since Mark Seavers, Ruby's father. "I'm Jen."

"Jen," he said softly as if he liked the way it rolled across his tongue.

Jen shifted her feet and glanced over his shoulder. "So how long are you in town for?"

"A while, I think. I'm actually looking for a place," he said and took another bite of his sandwich. He crunched on the freshly made potato chips, dipping them into the little bits of cheese that had spilled on the plate.

"Really? Well, if you want something in town, I know there are some new apartments down by the river." She grabbed a damp cloth and started wiping down the counter. He was one of her last lunch customers. The only folks left were sitting at the tables sipping cold coffee, taking advantage of the free Wi-Fi.

"Sounds expensive," he said.

She shrugged. "Mmm — maybe. I don't know what they're asking but you could check with Fibber's Realty down the street. They also do property management. They might have something they could show you."

"Thanks. I'll do that." He smiled his wide charming smile again. His bright blue eyes crinkled at the edges and her breath caught in her throat. Why on earth had she just thought him cute? He was downright handsome. "That's kind of an unfortunate name, isn't it? Fibber. Especially if you're trying to sell something."

She laughed, and it sounded too shrill in her ears. "Yeah, I guess. It's just everybody knows him, so—"

"So he's not a teller of fibs?" he said, cocking an eyebrow.

"No." She shook her head and rubbed her hand across her watch. "He plays it straight as an arrow." She grinned and shook her head, thinking of Ronny Fibber. He'd taken her to a seventh grade dance a hundred years ago and had kissed her chastely on the cheek at the end of the date. She looked down at the large silver watch face. 3 p.m. "Crap!"

He straightened up, mild surprise lining his face. "Something wrong?"

"I've gotta go," she said. "Is there anything else I can get you?"

"No, I'm good." He put up his hand and shook his head.

"Great. You can pay Dottie when you're ready." She jerked her thumb toward the older woman refilling sugar containers at the end of the counter. "You have a great day."

"Yeah, you too," he smiled. "Maybe I'll see you around sometime."

"Maybe." Jen giggled and was immediately disgusted with herself for turning into a fourteen-year-old girl. She slung her messenger bag across her body and headed out. When she glanced back over her shoulder at him he smiled and gave her a wave. Of course, he probably wouldn't be so eager to flirt if he knew she had a six-year-old kid and shared a house with her father.

* * *

As Jen swerved her ancient Ford F150 into the parking lot of Palmetto Point Elementary, she caught site of herself in the rearview mirror.

"Oh, brother," she muttered, finger-combing her dark, pixie haircut into something less bed-head and more responsible mother. Lilac shadows under her large blue eyes were not helping her cause, and she wished for just a second that she was one of those perfectly coiffed moms that came into the cafe mid-morning with their friends to talk about the latest book they'd read.

Most of the traffic had cleared out by the time she pulled up in front of the school. Not a good sign. She scanned the covered walkway for her daughter and saw her standing next to an adult. She sighed. Melinda Helms. Jen put the truck in park, and got out to retrieve her daughter.

"Hi, Melinda." Jen raised her hand to wave. Melinda bent down close to Ruby, whispering something into her ear. Ruby came running.

"Mommy! Where were you?" Ruby sounded panicked. Jen had been late before. What on earth had Melinda said to her daughter to get her all riled?

"I'm sorry, baby." Jen bent down and enveloped Ruby in her arms. "I had a customer at the last minute."

"That's okay, Mama. Camille and her mama stayed with me." Ruby pulled out of her mother's arms and gazed up at her. Jen ran the back of her knuckles across her daughter's round cheek. Sometimes it was like looking at a photograph of herself when she was that age. Ruby let out an audible sigh. "The chickens died."

"I know. We're gonna have a long talk about it on the way home, okay?"

"Okay."

"Hi." Melinda practically sung the announcement of her arrival. "Little Ruby was just waiting here all by herself, so Camille and I decided that it would be best to wait with her till her mommy came. Bless her heart, she was so scared that you weren't gonna come."

"Is that true? You were scared?" Jen asked.

Ruby's eyes flitted to Melinda and back to Jen. Her little voice shook as she whispered, "No."

Jen took a deep breath and centered herself. She kissed Ruby on the cheek, forced a smile to stretch her lips and stood up. "Well, thank you so much,

Melinda. Ruby knows that I would come and get her no matter what. I've never left her here before to fend for herself overnight or anything."

Melinda's tittering laugh was filled with the contempt that only southern women seem to be able to have for each other. "We'll bless your heart, of course you haven't. It must be so hard taking care of this little girl all by yourself and run that diner. It makes me exhausted just thinking about it."

"I'm sure it does. How's Josh?" Jen said, glancing at Melinda's left hand. The ginormous diamond ring was missing, replaced by a simple pearl ring on a thin gold band.

"Oh, he's fine." Melinda's voice sounded as strained as the smile painted across her face. "Well, we should get going. Camille has ballet at four." Melinda grabbed her daughter's hand and rushed off for the parking lot.

Ruby looked up with her large blue eyes. "Camille's daddy moved out, Mommy."

"Uh huh, I figured," Jen muttered, watching the Cadillac SUV pull away. "Fine my ass."

"Mommy," Ruby scolded. "Don't you already owe the swear jar twenty dollars?"

Jen sighed. "Well, now it looks like I owe it twenty-one. Come on, let's get you home before your granddaddy thinks we've run away and joined the circus."

Ruby giggled. The pair climbed into Jen's old truck and headed to her father's house. Poor old Melinda. Bless her heart. It just reminded Jen that not everything was as it seemed. Even perfect facades could crack and often did when least expected.

CHAPTER 3

On Tuesday morning, Deputy Jason Tate sat at the counter in the Kitchen Witch Café sipping the best coffee he'd ever tasted. It was 6:45 AM, and it had become his ritual to stop here on his way into the office to have a little breakfast. The café was a bustling place, full of people eating breakfast, ordering coffee, and muffins, and pancakes. He liked to sit at the end of the counter and just watch the people come and go. The energy of the sunny yellow walls and funky retro artwork calmed him. He had become addicted to it.

Jen Holloway stepped in front of him holding a steaming coffee carafe. The petite brunette smiled wide, her white teeth sparkling. "Well, good morning, Jason. More coffee?"

"That would be great," he said, pushing his half-empty cup across the counter. She tipped the carafe and the hot black liquid filled his cup.

"Did you order breakfast?" she asked.

"Yeah, I'm just getting a breakfast sandwich." He glanced down the counter toward Dottie the waitress. The older woman had one hand perched on her ample hips and held a carafe of coffee in the other. Her pale red hair was streaked with blond and held off her face with a headscarf. She smiled as she talked to another patron, filling his coffee cup.

"Okay, I just wanted to make sure you were taken care of," she said.

"I appreciate that," he said. It was one of the reasons why he loved this place — they took such good care of him here and the food was always delicious no matter what dish he tried. There were of course favorites of his on the menu. He saved the sausage gravy and biscuits for mornings when he had time to just sit and enjoy his meal. On payday he would order the steak and eggs. And the muffins. The tender-crumbed muffins, well he loved those anytime. Both the traditional and non-traditional flavors — blueberry streusel, cherry lime, lemon poppy-seed and pumpkin pecan pie muffins — all made his mouth water any time of the day. Strawberries N' Cream, in its pride of place at the top of the menu, was a particular favorite.

He doctored his coffee with a splash of milk and a

packet of sugar and thought about ordering some muffins to go.

"So you think Charlie'll be in this morning?"

"Um, I don't know." Jen's lips twisted into a knowing smile and she shrugged. "She has Evan this week, so it's hard to say. Do you have a case you want her to look at? I'll see her at dinner for sure."

"That's all right." He took a sip of his coffee. "I'll just text her later."

A shadow crossed Jen's wide blue eyes and all the good humor in her smile drained away as she scanned the room.

A cold finger touched Jason's heart and he instinctively followed her gaze across the busy café. "Everything okay?"

He'd only known Jen a little less than a year and he'd learned the hard way that even though she wasn't psychic the way her cousin Charlie was, she sensed things about the world. Things he could never sense — even with hyper-vigilance about his surroundings. He had come to trust her instinct, almost as much as he trusted Charlie's. Almost as much as he trusted his own.

Jen blinked long and slow. She took a deep breath and when she looked into his face again, the tension in her heart-shaped face softened. She smiled, but it seemed hollow and forced. "You're gonna want to get your food to go."

He opened his mouth to ask what she meant. He had plenty of time before he started his shift, but his cell phone rang. A photo of his partner Marshal Beck flipping the bird at him popped up on the screen. He pressed the green answer icon on his phone and watched as Jen went to the pass through where the food from the kitchen waited to be delivered to the hungry customers by a server. She took the sausage, egg and cheese biscuit from the plate sitting on the metal ledge, wrapped it in white waxy paper and stuffed it into a brown paper bag with the Kitchen Witch logo printed on it.

"Hey where are you?" Marshall Beck's voice filled his ear.

"Getting my breakfast. Where are you?"

"We got a situation. I need you to get out to Seward Nature Preserve."

"What kind of situation?" Dread, quiet and cold, slithered into his chest.

"We got a body. And it's—" Marshall Beck paused and cleared his throat. Jason had never heard him sound so shaken in the three years that they had worked together. Beck had been a deputy for almost seventeen years and had done special investigations for ten of that. There wasn't much that got to him.

"It's what?"

"It's bad—" the pause stretched out and for a long

second Jason thought the call had dropped. "It's the most gruesome thing I think I've ever seen."

"All right, I'm on my way," Jason said firmly. Images of past crime scenes filtered through his head. How bad was bad? He reached into his back pocket for his wallet. Jen placed a paper bag and a to-go cup of coffee down in front of him.

"Put your wallet away. You know family doesn't pay here." She pushed the coffee toward him. "Just a splash of milk and one sugar, right?"

Jason looked up at her, his gaze meeting hers. For a brief second, looking into Jen's soft elfin face, the dark images fled his head, leaving behind only a sense of calm and purpose. How did she do that?

"Right," he croaked. He pulled three one-dollar bills from his wallet and put them under his cup. "Thanks."

"Sure." She gave him a solemn smile. "You're still wearing your pendant, right?"

Jason's fingers twitched, but he fought the urge to reach for the small silver pentacle hanging around his neck. He wore it every day, the same way he wore a bulletproof vest. The hair on the back of his neck stood at attention. Why would she ask that?

"Good," she said. "Call us if you need us. Okay?"

"Thank you. I appreciate that." He offered up a smile, grabbed his coffee and the bag of breakfast then headed out.

* * *

BY THE TIME HE PULLED INTO THE PARKING LOT OF THE
Seward Nature Preserve and Education Center, two
other deputy cruisers and the coroner's van had
arrived.

The nature preserve was part of an old rice plan-
tation. It was surrounded by water, wetlands and
long abandoned rice fields. Walking trails and board-
walks crisscrossed the sixteen-acre property, and it
had become a prime spot for birdwatchers and
nature lovers. Jason pulled his black Dodge Charger
up next to Beck's cruiser and surveyed the situation.

The windows of the small brick building looked
dark. No doubt the education center was locked up
tight. Anything a person wanted to learn about rice
fields — how they worked and the economy of the
area when rice was still king of the cash crops — this
was the place. Sometimes on Saturdays he'd come
out here and walk the trails. It was quiet and peaceful
and on a good day he would see ospreys and even
the occasional bald eagle.

An older man with silver hair stood in front of
Beck. He was tall and thin and wore cargo pants.
An expensive looking pair of binoculars hung
around his neck and his companion, an older
woman in khaki long pants and a pink plaid shirt
was holding an expensive DSLR with a long lens.

They both looked pale and shaken as Beck questioned them.

Jason took one last sip of his coffee and climbed out of his car to join his partner. He caught Beck's eye and gave him a nod. Then headed toward one of the deputies who was carrying a role of yellow police tape.

"Hey, McCleary—" Jason said as he approached.

The young deputy who could not have been more than twenty-two turned and faced him.

"Lieutenant," McCleary said.

"What's going on? Where's the body?"

McCleary pointed toward the boardwalk that headed off into a cypress bog. "Couple of birdwatchers found him this morning."

"Take me to him," Jason said.

"Sure thing," the deputy said. They headed off down the path to the boardwalk that wound through the cypress bog over the black water.

"Do we know what happened?"

"Something pretty fucked up, sir," Deputy McCleary said.

"What do you mean?" Jason asked, but before McCleary could answer they had already arrived at the spot where two deputies were pulling on waterproof rubber chest waders. Another two deputies nearby were loading hunting rifles. A low growl resonated across the shallow water. Jason stopped in his tracks when he saw the body suspended from a branch of a cypress tree. The man hung upside-down in midair with his arms stretched out toward the water and it was apparent that the gator had already taken a swipe at him. Part of one of the man's arms was gone leaving behind only ragged flesh. A large gash across his forehead dripped blood into the black water below. A dinner bell for just about every gator in the park.

The water couldn't have been more than a few feet deep, but an alligator had parked himself underneath the body ready to defend his perceived catch. The gator looked to be at least twelve feet long and his dark, beady eyes watched the men, safe, out of his reach. Jason scanned the swamp, surprised there weren't more gators. *They're there, you just can't see them.* Every hair on the back of his neck stood up at that thought.

Sheriff Rex T. Bedford stood talking to the coroner. He had his hands on his hips and a grim look on his thin, leathery face. The two men kept pointing to the gator.

"Good morning, sirs," Jason said as he approached.

"Deputy Tate," the sheriff said.

"Any idea how this happened?"

The sheriff narrowed his eyes and scowled at Jason. Not a good sign this early in the morning.

"Well from the looks of it, this fool was trying to bait gators. Your partner thinks the fool tied the rope to the tree and tossed it over that branch. See the rope wrapped around his foot?" The Sherriff pointed to the body. "There's also a big old hook buried deep in his calf. Beck thinks he got his foot tangled in the rope and somehow put the boat in gear and hit his head and ended up swinging above the water."

"Did we find the boat?" Jason scanned the immediate area.

"Yep, 'bout a hundred yards that way." The sheriff pointed deeper into the swamp. "Also found a cooler full of beer and four whole chickens."

"Kinda brave to gator hunt in a nature preserve."

"That's one word for it," the sheriff said dryly.

"Is there a plan in place yet for getting the body down?"

"Yep. Very cautiously." The sheriff put his hands on his hips just below his apparent love handles.

"Yes, sir," Jason said. "We gonna kill the gator?"

"Maybe," the sheriff said. "I have no love for the damned things but some of my tree-hugging, love-all-the-animals constituents do."

"Yes, sir," Jason nodded. "The media may not be kind, especially since this gator's in his own habitat and not swimming in someone's pool."

The coroner smirked. "And next year's an election year, isn't that right, Rex?"

The sheriff cast a dirty look at the coroner, but the man didn't seem to care.

"Maybe we could scare him off with a couple of boats and enough noise," Jason offered. He hated to see any animal die unnecessarily, especially when it was just doing what animals do. The humans were the invaders here, not the other way around. But he couldn't say that out loud to his boss.

"Or we could just shoot the damned thing," Beck said as he approached them. "Who's gonna tell the media? I'm not. None of these guys are." He gestured to the other deputies.

The sheriff scowled, and his thin lips disappeared beneath the silver hair of his mustache.

Jason threw a dirty look at his partner and knelt at the edge of the boardwalk. He looked into the animal's black eyes. *Go on now fella, you're not gonna get any breakfast here.* The animal emitted a low growl and Jason could almost feel the vibration in his bones. *Come on now. Get out of here. Before somebody takes a gun to you.* The twelve-footer's tail swished, splashing the water around him and suddenly he submerged beneath the dark water.

"Where the hell did he go?" Beck asked.

"They spend more time underneath the water than on top of it. Unless they're sunning on a bank," Jason said. He stood up and put his hands on his hips and faced his partner.

"How do you know?" Beck asked.

"I happen to have gone through the nature center before. You'd know that too if you'd ever done anything to educate yourself."

"Do you think he's just down there? Lying in wait?" Beck asked.

"I don't know." Jason glanced back at the spot where the gator had been floating beneath the body. "Maybe. Or maybe he just decided he didn't have much of a chance of getting a meal."

"Well, either way," the sheriff interjected. "We still need to get that body down so we can start our investigation. I'm going to go handle the press."

"Yes, sir," Jason said.

"Yes, sir." Beck glanced over his shoulder.

The sheriff walked away, his heavy boots sounding hollow against the gray wood of the boardwalk. When his gaze shifted from their boss back to Jason, Beck wore a smirk on his thick lips. "Nice jewelry."

"What are you talking about?" Jason said.

Beck pointed to his neck. "What is that? Some sort of star? Did you convert to Judaism all of a sudden?"

Jason scrambled to put the pendant that had slipped out, back inside his undershirt.

"Not your damn business. And I was gonna ask if you all of a sudden converted to being an asshole but I already know the answer to that."

Beck made an amused sound in the back of his throat and smirked. "Come on let's get this done."

Jason watched the two deputies wearing waders slip into the thigh-high water. The other two deputies moved to the edge of the boardwalk with their rifles ready in case the alligator returned. The pendant Jason wore suddenly felt warm against the skin of his upper chest and he touched his hand to it through his shirt. Two more deputies arrived with the canoe. They slid it onto the boardwalk and into the water and the deputies slipped in without making a splash and guided it toward the tree where the body was suspended.

Jason scanned the trees. "We should find out what's the easiest routes into the nature preserve from the river or one of the marshes."

"What are you thinking?" Beck asked.

"I doubt this guy came in through the front gate of the nature preserve. Maybe his car is parked at one of the nearby public landings."

"Yeah, that's definitely a possibility. The question is why here? I mean what kind of idiot sets up gator lines in a well-known nature preserve? What's the point?"

"You got me," Jason said. "People have done stupider shit that's gotten them killed. We should still probably check and see if there's a video feed. Maybe he's been here before scoping out the place. I spotted some cameras on the building when I came in."

"Yep. I'm already on it. As soon as the manager of the nature site gets here, I'll collect it."

They watched as two deputies held the canoe beneath the body. One deputy took a knife from his pocket and sawed through the rope tied around the base of the tree. The body fell with a thud, crashing into the metal canoe. Jason winced at the hollow sound. Beck pulled two pairs of gloves from his front pocket and handed a pair to Jason. Once the divers had retrieved the body, they guided the long green boat back to the boardwalk. It took five men to lift and maneuver the canoe with the body onto the boardwalk. The coroner performed an obligatory pronouncement of death and Jason slid his hands into his gloves and he and Beck began to gather any evidence.

Beck knelt next to the canoe and dug through the man's pants pockets. "I got a wallet." He opened the brown folded leather and pulled the license from behind a window of clear plastic. "His name's Tony Smoak."

"Does he have anything else?"

"Yeah." Beck made a face as he reached deeper into the man's front pocket and pulled out a short string of black and white beads. A crushed feather hung on by a thread of what appeared to be hair. Beck held it up to his face. "What the hell?"

"What is it?"

Beck inspected the beads more closely. "Holy shit, there are symbols carved into some of these. This looks like some hoodoo shit."

"Lemme see." Jason took the strand of beads from his partner and ran his fingers over some of the symbols. He only recognized one of them. A five-sided star like the one on his necklace.

"Your psychic friend know anything about hoodoo?"

Jason scowled. "I don't know. Maybe."

"Figures."

"Shut up and hand me an evidence bag," Jason said pulling his phone from his front pocket. Beck turned to one of the other deputies and snapped his fingers. Jason glared at him. "You know you could just ask."

"Why? He knew what I meant, didn't you Deputy?" Beck jerked his thumb toward McCleary.

McCleary gave Jason a long-suffering look and nodded his head. He took one of the clear baggies with the word evidence printed on it and handed it to Jason. "Yes, sir."

"Thank you," Jason said. He slipped the beads into the baggie, then held it up and took a picture of it.

"You are gonna show that to that psychic of yours, aren't you?" Beck asked, his voice laced with disapproval.

Jason frowned. "Not every case involves Charlie. But I want a picture of it while I'm doing my research on it."

Beck rolled his eyes. "Sure, whatever man." Beck jerked his thumb toward the boardwalk heading back to the nature center. "I'm gonna head back and give a friend of mine with DNR a call to see if he has any maps of the area."

"You don't even have to go that far — the nature center has maps of the property and the whole area," Jason said.

"How do you know that?" Beck asked.

"You've never been through the nature center?" Jason asked.

"No. Why would I?"

"Maybe 'cause it's interesting," Jason said with a snarky tone.

"Well, I'm just a dumb old redneck hick. I'm not all edumacated like you," Beck shot back, making his accent thicker.

Jason laughed. "Fuck you. Go on. I'll check in with you later."

Beck nodded and headed back toward the parking lot.

Jason waited until his partner was out of sight

before he whipped off a quick text to Charlie and attached the photo.

* * *

CHARLIE PRESSED THE BUTTON ON HER PHONE ENDING her last call and then punched in the four digits for the wrap code indicating she was going to lunch. She grabbed her cell phone from the keyboard tray and glanced at the screen. She had one text. From Jason. She glanced around, surveying her co-workers. They were all on the phone, talking to each other or in a wrap code finishing up their last call. She opened the bottom drawer of her desk and pulled out her purse, tucking her phone into the side pocket.

"I'll see you in thirty," she said to her co-worker Brian. He looked up from his call and gave her a little salute, then continued with his call.

Once she left the call center and headed for the large break room, Charlie pulled her phone from her purse and opened the text and read it. She stopped in her tracks and whipped off her answer. Unlike her son, she had not mastered the ability to text and walk. She tucked the phone into the back pocket of her black pants and continued on to the break room.

She grabbed her bag out of one of the three refrigerators and chose a diet soda from the vending machine. It was almost three p.m. and she had the break room to herself. She pulled her phone from her pants and laid it on the table next to her lunch bag and began to pull out her salad in a jar and her strawberry yogurt. Her phone beeped and vibrated on the tabletop, startling her. She turned it over and read the one word text. It said: *Weirdness.* His response to her question of why he needed her. A moment later a photo appeared. She touched it and it filled the small screen of her smart phone. Another text.

Do you know what this is?

She opened the photo again and looked over the object - a string of knotted beads. She zoomed in and counted forty knots. Some beads were large and grayish white and reminded her of carved bone. Feathers had been attached to the string by what she thought looked like hair.

It looks like a Witch's Ladder but my cousin Jen or my aunt Evangeline will know for sure.

What is it for?

It's used as part of a spell. Where did you get it?

I found it on a body.

How did he/she die?

The verdict is still out on that but the coroner thinks it's probably from a head injury. Won't know for sure until the autopsy is complete. Why?

Did you touch it?

The body? Yes.

NO. The beads. Did you touch the beads with your bare hands or gloved?

They're evidence. Gloved of course.

Good. Have the coroner check it for drugs. Specifically hallucinogenic drugs. Something that could be absorbed through skin.

WTH????!

If it's a Witch's Ladder it's used to curse someone. As a back up to the curse, it's_common to dip the beads in poison or drugs that could either kill directly, or lead to hallucinations which often cause accidents that would lead to death. But even if it tests negative for those things, DO NOT touch it with bare skin. We don't know if we're dealing with a witch or just someone screwing around with something they shouldn't be.

OK. What does that mean? You think it's really cursed?

You have a dead body, right?

Yeah, so? Who's to say this guy didn't just whack his head and fall into the water?

He could have. It could have totally been an accident. OR he could've been cursed.

Charlie watched the screen. Waiting for any sign that he was responding. A few seconds later the word OK appeared. No questions asked. No arguing. They'd come a long way in the ten months they'd known each other.

* * *

CHARLIE HUNG UP THE PHONE AND ENTERED THE FOUR-digit code signing her off for the day. She carefully removed her headset and hung it on the hook on her desk before tidying up her work space and logging out of her computer for the day. When she stood, she slung her purse across her body and waved goodbye to her cube mate Brian.

She stepped out of the Belcom Credit Union call center building and breathed in the early evening air stretching her back and noticing the sky, streaks of pink and orange melding into purple. This was her favorite time of day when the world was cast in that milky haze of twilight. She headed to the employee parking lot that was separated from the highway by a thick growth of pine trees. She pulled her keys from her purse and as she got closer to her car, she pressed the unlock button on her key fob. Her lights blinked, and the car made a loud chirping sound. The wind kicked up and something cold settled around her shoulders. The hair on the back of her neck stood at attention and Charlie slowed her pace, suddenly aware that she was not alone. Only one thing in the world made her skin prickle this way. A ghost. Charlie glanced around, suspicious of every shadow, every flicker of light.

She quickened her pace, in line with her heart,

which beat like a thunderous drum in her ears. The hairs on her arms stood at attention, her whole body twitched as if someone had pressed a live wire to her skin. Whatever it was, wherever it was, she could feel it growing closer, watching her. The question was why. Spirits often sought her out. It was like once they were dead, her name got passed around. *Find Charlie Payne — she can help you.* And she certainly didn't have a problem helping the dead, but she didn't like being watched.

When she got to her car, she opened the door and hopped inside, pressing the lock button immediately. Then she laughed at herself. There were no door locks that would keep the spirit out. It hadn't even occurred to her to spirit-proof her car. She would get on that when she got home. She put her key into the ignition and turned it. She began to adjust the rearview mirror. The sight of him sitting in her back seat made her breath catch in her throat. When she looked more carefully at his face, she recognized him immediately. He was the man from the parking lot. The one looking for his stepdaughter.

"Who are you?" Charlie asked.

The spirit leered at her. "Oh, you know who I am."

"Do you know what's happened to you?"

"Yeah," he said flatly. His brown eyes darkened. "You killed me."

"What are you talking about?"

"It's your fault I'm dead. I figured you killed me, I guess that means I get to kill you. You stupid meddling witch."

Charlie had opened her mouth to protest but something clamped down on her throat, making it impossible to breathe. Her gaze met his as she clawed at her neck trying to fight off the invisible fingers squeezing the life out of her. The world began to swim and the weight on Charlie's neck and chest grew heavier. This is not how she wanted to die. There were so many things still left to do. The image of her son popped into her head. How would she ever see Evan fully grow into the man he was supposed to be without her? The next image was of Tom, which surprised her? Surely she was beyond oxygen-deprived to be thinking of Tom Sharon, a man who was not even a man but a reaper who cast a glamour to walk among the humans and cull the dead.

She had forgiven him for a lie he'd told her and they'd started to rebuild their friendship over the past couple of months. Her heart suddenly ached, and she wasn't sure if it was because her body was dying or because she would no longer get to see and talk to Tom. Her nails dug into the skin of her neck drawing blood but it didn't loosen the spirits crushing grip.

"Pluh-please," she managed to croak.

Hot tears squeezed out of her eyes and trailed down her cheeks. "I have a son." She didn't know how much longer she could last. "Please."

A sound burst into her consciousness. It wasn't a growl exactly. More of a vibration. It started inside her head growing louder and more fierce. Her head was thrust backwards into the headrest and then forward, knocking so hard into the steering wheel a great bloom of red sparks appeared in her vision. Darkness flooded over her and right before she sank into tarry unconsciousness she felt something icy cold whisper across the skin near her ear, "I'll be watching you."

* * *

CHARLIE STARED AT THE SPECKLED WHITE CEILING TILES of the corridor as the orderly wheeled her down the hall back toward the ER. Her hand kept touching the brace supporting her neck. The doctor had ordered the CT scan because the EMT's had found her unconscious.

No one seemed to believe her when she squeaked out that she was just fine. They'd done an X-ray on her neck and though it was bruised, nothing was broken. The doctors kept telling her to stop trying to talk. Finally, someone had given her a pad and pen and she had written — *I make my living talking. How long?*

The young, handsome doctor with blue shadows beneath his eyes had only answered, "The more you try to talk the longer it will take." So she laid still and said nothing more.

"Okay, Miss Payne," the orderly said as he brought her back to the emergency room. He looked at the nursing station and a woman wearing scrubs and holding a phone to her ear directed him into one of the tiny rooms.

"Here we are," he said as he transferred her to the ER bed. "One of the nurses will be with you Stat."

Charlie started to write down a question, but he disappeared into the surrounding chaos before she could finish it. There were bruises on her neck and a black and blue goose egg on her forehead. The doctors and nurses all believed she'd been attacked, choked in her car by a man hiding in the back. She heard two nurses whisper about what they thought happened to her. Charlie hated the idea of being a cautionary tale. A reminder to lock their doors and look over their shoulders in dark parking lots.

The only thing that could have made the ER worse would have been for the spirits roaming the hall to home in on her. Maybe it was not such a bad thing that she couldn't talk. Then she could just pretend the spirits weren't there and they would give up and go away.

A ruckus caught her attention, and a burly voice she recognized immediately carried across the emergency room. Her heart lightened. The cavalry had come to free her from this awful place.

"You know I still have privileges at this hospital young lady," the voice said. "Now why don't you get Dr. Handleman on the phone and tell him Jack Holloway needs some help down in the E.R."

Charlie couldn't help but smile.

"Now where is my niece?"

The nurse fumbled with her roster and then pointed.

"Hey there darlin'," her uncle said, poking his head into her tiny room. Jack Holloway stepped inside the room and immediately picked up her chart. An old habit, Charlie figured, from his days as a doctor.

Charlie pointed to her throat had made a cutting gesture across her neck as she wrote down her hello on the pad the hospital had given her.

"Am I going to live?" Charlie handed the pad to her uncle, and he chuckled. Jen craned her neck and read over her father's elbow.

"Oh my gosh. Of course you're going to live," Jen said, pushing in front of her father. "Oh your poor neck. Are you in much pain?"

Charlie shook her head no. Then wrote, "Only when I talk. Where's Evan?"

"I know it'll be hard but you'll just have to keep quiet for a day or two," Jack teased.

Charlie made an exaggerated frown face.

Jen rolled her eyes at her father. "Don't worry. I called Scott, told him what happened. He's gonna keep Evan with him until you're better."

Jack added, "You'll be right as rain in a couple of days and can pick him up then."

Charlie scribbled quickly on her notepad, "Is that your official diagnosis?"

He smirked. "Of course."

"Hello, folks," Deputy Billy Eisener stood in the doorway, with his gray felted hat in his hand. Jen and Jack both turned at the same time. Her uncle and cousin stepped back from her bedside.

"Hey Jen. Hey Dr. Holloway. Hey Charlie." Billy sidled up next to Charlie on the other side of the bed. "Looks like somebody did a number on you."

Charlie sighed and nodded. She just didn't know how to tell him that it was a ghost that did it. She quickly wrote, "Are you here to take my statement? Where is Jason Tate?"

Billy read her note and nodded his head. He always reminded Charlie of a basset hound with his long face and dark, soulful brown eyes. "I am." He pulled a notepad from his front breast pocket, along with a silver ballpoint pen. "I think Jason's off duty already."

A soft pang in her heart made Charlie touch her fingers to her breastbone.

"You all right?" Billy asked.

Charlie gently tapped her fingers against her solar plexus and gave him a weak smile and mouthed, "I'm fine."

Billy poised his pen against his notepad. "So, what do you remember?"

Charlie put her pen against the paper trying to decide exactly how much of the truth to tell him. If Jason had come, she wouldn't have to be lying to the police, but she didn't want anybody wasting their time trying to find her attacker when she was the only one who could see him. *Me and maybe Tom*, she thought. Another soft pang squeezed her heart.

She wrote, "I didn't get a good look at him. He was in the backseat. All I remember is starting my car and then being choked. I must've passed out."

"Well, your purse and the other valuables were still in the car when we got to the scene. So it doesn't appear to be a robbery. There anybody that you can think of that might be upset with you or—" Billy gave her a sheepish look. "Do you have any enemies, Charlie?"

Charlie's eyes widened at the question. Did she have any enemies? Obviously none that were human.

She shrugged her shoulders and shook her head to indicate that she didn't know.

"Yeah, that's what I thought," Billy said.

"Billy," Jen said. "Maybe you should check with the bank and see if they have any cameras."

"Oh, yeah that's a great idea," Billy said scribbling it down his notepad. "Charlie do you know if they have security cameras in the parking lot where you work?"

Charlie nodded and pressed her lips together to keep from smiling. Bless Billy's heart, he wasn't the sharpest tool in the shed, that was for sure. It made her long for Jason to be asking her these questions.

Charlie scribbled down a name in her pad and tore out the sheet and pushed it toward Billy.

"Is this the person I should talk to?" Billy asked.

Charlie nodded. She really could see why Lisa would prefer Jason over Billy. Not that she approved.

"Okay. Well I'll pull the video and see what we can find out. Maybe we can find this guy breaking into your car."

Jen patted Billy on the shoulder. "That would be great. How are you doing, Billy?"

"I'm doing fine. How about you, Jen?"

"So, same old, same old."

"All right, well now we all know that we're doing fine," Jack interrupted. "There anything else you need here, Billy? Because we'd like to get this little lady discharged and home where she can be comfortable."

"No, sir. I think I've got everything I need. Thank you."

"Alrighty then. You have a good night, Billy."

"Yes sir." Billy closed his notebook and slipped it and his pen back into his front breast pocket. "Y'all have a good night." Billy headed toward the door then turned around abruptly as if he had forgotten something. "Oh yeah, Charlie, if you remember anything else, you know, don't hesitate to call me here, okay?"

Billy pulled a card from his front pocket and slipped it into Charlie's hand. She took it and held it close to her chest.

"Thank you," she mouthed.

"You take care of yourself, Charlie." Billy gave her a quick nod and a smile. "It was good to see you, Jen. You too, Dr. Holloway." He turned and left the room. Jen let out a loud breath.

"Wow. I did not expect to see Billy Eisener today."

"I never expect to see Billy Eisener," Jack quipped. He reached over and gave Charlie's foot a gentle squeeze. "I'm gonna go see if I can figure out what's taking your doctor so long. I'm sure you're ready to get out of here."

Charlie gave her uncle a soft smile. Jack winked at her and disappeared into the middle of the ER chaos.

"I think he misses coming to the hospital every day," Jen said thoughtfully as she watched her father mill around the nursing station.

Charlie quickly scribbled onto her notepad, "Would you do me a favor?"

Jen took the pad and read it. "Anything, sweetie."

Charlie wrote, "Would you please text Jason and tell him what's happened?"

"Of course," Jen said. "Is there anything else?"

Charlie shook her head no and laid her head back on the pillow. It was on the tip of her tongue to ask if Jen knew anything about Lisa and Jason but she didn't have the energy to write it out. Instead she closed her eyes and whispered, "I'm just gonna rest a minute."

"Good idea." Jen patted Charlie's leg and sat down in the plastic and metal chair near the bed. "I'll be right here if you need me."

CHAPTER 4

C harlie curled up on the couch in her tiny living room, her head and throat aching dully. She rested on one of the big, fluffy floral pillows with her head cradled in her elbow and the remote control to her TV nestled in her other hand. The discharge sheets from the hospital were laid out in front of her on the trunk that she used as a coffee table. Along with a bottle of aspirin and a large glass of ice water. The ice had mostly melted. Charlie knew she should finish it up and just go to bed; it was getting late. She finally had to kick Jen out an hour ago. She flicked the television off and pushed herself up to a sitting position. She stood up and grabbed her glass and the bottle of aspirin and headed toward the kitchen. She took two aspirin from the bottle and washed them down with a large swallow of the cold water before emptying the glass in the sink, giving it a quick scrub with the brush and leaving it to dry in the drainer on the counter. The knock on the door made her stop in her tracks. She rolled her eyes.

"Dammit, Jen," she muttered under her breath as she walked to the front door. Charlie flipped on the porch light and pushed the eyelet curtain aside and peered through the window. Her eyes widened, and she quickly undid the deadbolt. She pulled open the door and found Tom Sharon standing on her top step.

"I come bearing gifts," he said. He held up a paper bag with the Kitchen Witch logo on the side. "Chicken soup. I hear it's the best in the county and cures what ever ails you."

He smiled and Charlie couldn't help but be enchanted by his charm. She touched her palm to her face then shifted it to cover her throat. "Tom," she whispered hoarsely. "I look so awful."

Tom smiled. "You look fine. You've been through an ordeal."

"How did you even..." Charlie rasped, but she already knew the answer.

Tom shrugged. "It's a small town." He smiled slyly. "And Jen texted me."

"Right. Jen," Charlie whispered, nodding. She took a step back and gestured for him to come inside.

"I don't want to keep you. She told me you can't really talk, but I did want to check on you. See if you're all right and see if I could help. Since your attacker was—"

Tears stung the back of her throat and Charlie clenched her jaw to stop herself from crying. Jen had asked her if she was all right a hundred times tonight and every time she had sighed and nodded her head and scribbled, "I'm fine, really," onto a pad.

She should've answered Tom the same way. They were friends again, and she enjoyed his company tremendously. But when he asked if she was all right, she could not find the words to answer because saying, "I'm fine," would have been a lie.

"It's all right," Tom said. He placed a hand on one of her shoulders and gave it a gentle squeeze. "I can see that you're not. Why don't you have a seat? I'm going to put this in the kitchen. Unless you'd like some now."

Charlie shook her head, afraid if she whispered one word she would burst into tears. Tom offered her a smile but there was no pity in his eyes and for that she was thankful. She sat back down on her couch and grabbed one of the small, solid-colored pillows, hugging it to her chest. She listened as Tom opened the refrigerator and put the soup inside. It was strangely comforting to have him here.

"I'm sorry I didn't come sooner," Tom said.

"Where should I put this paper bag? Never mind, don't answer. I see you have a basket for them on the top of the refrigerator."

Charlie smiled as she listened to him fold it up and slide it into the basket. A moment later he turned the corner with a wide smile on his handsome face. "Is there anything else I can do for you?"

Charlie shrugged her shoulders and croaked out, "Yeah."

"What?"

"Could you stand guard?" Her voice broke on the last word. The tears hit her harder than she ever expected. She leaned forward and put her hands over her face.

"Oh my God, Charlie. Come here," he said, taking a seat beside her and wrapping an arm around her shoulders. She let him pull her to him and she buried her face against his shoulder. She wept, letting all the fear and confusion and anger out.

"He said he'd be watching me," Charlie whispered.

"This place is locked up tight, Charlie. Jen and Evangeline have seen to that. No spirit is going to get to you here."

"He can't cross the boundary but he can get to me in my dreams." Charlie pulled away from him and looked him in the eye.

Tom pushed a stray hair behind her ear. "I can stay if you want. Stand guard all night."

She hesitated, clearing her throat, making it ache more. "I was only half-way joking. It's a lot to ask."

"Only if you're human, which I'm not. It's not as if I need to sleep."

Charlie sniffed and gazed into his golden brown eyes. His breath was sweet and warm on her face. "I've always wondered about that."

Tom smiled and brushed a tear from her cheek. "You know you are welcome to ask me any questions about that sort of thing. It won't bother me in the least."

"Thank you. I'll keep that in mind." Charlie forced herself to sit back further, fighting the natural magnetism between the two of them. He was not human, she reminded herself. She could not allow herself to love him. She smiled weakly and touched her throat. Tom nodded as if he'd read her mind.

"Well, I guess I'll be going then. But I won't be too far. If I'm out of this skin and you call my name aloud, I'll come."

"How often are you out of your skin?" Charlie asked.

Tom smiled slyly but didn't answer.

"What? You said I could ask."

He pursed his lips and chuckled. "More often than I'm in it. How's that for an answer?"

71

"I'll take what I can get." Charlie pushed to her feet and crossed her arms. "Thank you for the soup and for the breakdown."

Tom stood up and put his hand on her upper arm. "Any time. Remember what I said."

"I will. Thank you," she croaked.

* * *

CHARLIE HEARD CLUCKING, AND IT ROUSED HER FROM her sleep. At first she thought she was dreaming when she sat up and found Penny the chicken roosting on her footboard. Charlie sat up in bed and stared at the apparition of the chicken.

"I still don't know how I'm going to help you," she said, her voice raspy and sore-sounding. She touched her neck, and the muscle was still tender but it felt as if some of the swelling had gone down. She got up and dressed. Then ambled into the kitchen to make coffee. The wood floor was cold beneath her feet. She took the carafe from the coffee maker and filled it up with water. She glanced out the window toward the wide expanse of green grass. The sun was not quite up yet and the soft layer of fog rippled across the wide expanse of grass. In the gray light near the edge of the woods she thought she saw Tom and his reaper form drifting like a black shadow along the boundary of trees. A soft breeze blew the

Spanish moss and she could almost see his robes ripple in the wind. He had stayed all night. Just as he had said he would. She wondered if it had been within his power to keep her from dreaming. And she made up her mind to ask him the next time she saw him. She finished filling the coffee maker with water and lined the inner chamber with a filter before scooping her dark Vienna roast into it and pressing the button. It gurgled and began to drip and she headed toward the bathroom to take a shower. A knock on the door startled her, and she grabbed a sweater off the hook by the front door and shoved her arms into it to cover up her tank top before opening it.

Jason Tate stood on her front stoop with a worried look etching deep lines into his face.

"Hey," she said.

"Why haven't you answered me?"

"What are you talking about?" she said in a froggy voice.

"I have been calling and texting you all night. I almost came over here. And I would have done if Jen hadn't told me not to. Can I come in?"

Charlie stood back and gestured for him to enter. He sauntered in, glancing around as if he were looking for something.

"Are you okay?" he asked. "I'm sorry I didn't get to the hospital before they discharged you."

"That's okay. I didn't expect you to come," she lied. "Do you want some coffee?"

"No," he said sounding agitated. "I want to know what happened."

"Well I want some coffee," she said. "And I'm not supposed to be talking a lot. I'm supposed to be resting my voice today. I have to call in a few minutes and let my supervisor know I'm not coming into work. And I need you to be quiet when I do that. God knows I don't want her to think I'm playing hooky."

"I'm sure nobody at your work thinks you are playing hooky. They should be praying that you're not going to sue them for not having a security guard walk you out."

"Security guard wouldn't of been able to help me," she scoffed. And headed back toward the kitchen. Jason followed her through the living room and into the small, cozy kitchen. Charlie pulled a mug down from one of the open shelves and poured herself a fresh cup of coffee. "Have a seat." She gestured to the small bistro table and grabbed the carton of half-and-half out of her refrigerator.

"Why wouldn't a security guard have been able to help you? You were attacked in their parking lot."

"Because I wasn't attacked by a human being. At least not a living one." Charlie poured a generous dollop of half-and-half into her coffee and then took four scoops of sugar from the pink sugar bowl on the table. When she looked up all the color had drained from Jason's face.

"Are you telling me a ghost did this?" he said, incredulous.

"That is exactly what I'm saying," she said, taking a long sip of her coffee. She closed her eyes and savored the bittersweet flavor.

"What the hell?" he said. "How could a ghost do that to you? You have physical bruises on your neck."

"I know," Charlie said. "He was pissed. He said I killed him. Which is ridiculous. He also said he would be watching me. Which is unnerving."

"Do you know who he was?" Jason asked, his tone softening.

"Sort of," Charlie said. "I was going to come talk to you about it today, actually."

"Who was it?"

"Remember I told you that I found that teenager in my car the other day?"

"Yeah," Jason said.

"It was her father. Which means that he's dead. The question I have is whether she had anything to do with it."

"Did he say anything to you about how he ended up dead?" Jason asked.

"Well, we didn't sit down and have a conversation, if that's what you're asking. He was a little busy concentrating all his energy on choking me to death."

"Could he have done that? Killed you?"

"I don't know. Maybe. I told him I had a son, and that made his energy falter. If he'd been a truly evil bastard then, maybe."

"He choked you. That makes him pretty freaking evil to me," Jason said.

"No. Not all spirits are evil. A lot of the time they're just misguided. He really did believe I killed him. I just don't know why."

"Do you think he'll come after you again?"

Charlie took in a deep breath and blew it out. "God, I hope not."

"Is there anything Jen or Evangeline can do?"

"This property already has wards all along the boundary."

"What does that mean? Wards?"

"They're basically objects that ward off evil spirits and demons. I don't even think vampires can penetrate the boundaries around this property."

"Okay, now you're just screwing with me."

"Okay," Charlie said, smirking. "Whatever you say. Anyway nothing outside this property is getting in. The only possible thing left for her to do would be to put a binding spell on the cottage. But that could be more trouble than it's worth. It could keep me from going out."

"Well I guess you know what's best." Jason sighed. "I guess you're probably not up for helping me, huh?"

Charlie shook her head and chuckled. "Let me call my boss and tell her that I'm not coming into work. And then I'm all yours."

"Then it will be like you really are playing hooky," Jason teased.

"Hush," she said. "Do you want me to help you or not?"

Jason held his hands up in surrender. "You know I do."

* * *

CHARLIE FOLLOWED JASON INTO THE SHERIFF'S STATION. She had carefully applied cover-up, powder to her throat and then tied a pretty yellow and green scarf around her neck to hide the bruises. The last thing she wanted was for Marshall Beck to give her a hard time. Jason signed her in and grabbed the working folder from his desk before ushering her into one of the nearby interrogation rooms. Charlie sat on one side and he sat on the other. He opened up the folder and slid a small plastic bag with the words Evidence printed on it across to her. Charlie's hand drifted to her throat and a feeling of nausea waved over her. Darkness emanated from the bag, glowing black and thick. There were so many emotions that swirled in that blackness. She didn't want to touch it. Even with it bound up in plastic.

"You okay?" Jason asked.

"Yeah," she said in a raspy whisper.

"You look like you just saw a ghost. And I mean that in the expression sense because you usually seem calm when you see ghosts. But now you just look pale and like you might throw up. You're not gonna throw up, are you?"

"You don't feel it?" she asked, meeting his gaze.

"Feel what?" Jason said, his voice sounding mesmerized.

"That object is cursed. It is—" she wrapped her arms around her torso and hugged herself tight. "For lack of a better word ... evil. It has one purpose, and that is to kill. It is glowing with death."

Jason shifted his gaze from her to the object and she could see him working over her words in his mind. Weighing them against what he knew and against what he felt.

"So if I touched it. It would kill me?"

"It's not as direct as that. Did you have them test it for poisons?"

"Yeah, they tested it for several things. So far they didn't find anything but some tests will take a few weeks to come back from the lab."

"I'm not really surprised about that I guess," she

said. "Can you just put it back in the folder to cover it up or something?"

Jason pulled a handkerchief out of his front pocket, unfolded it and placed it over the beads. "Better?"

"Better would be to take that and burn it. But that'll do for now," she said. "What else do you have for me?"

"Not much, really. Just the crime scene photos." He pushed the stack of photos over to her and she used one of them to push the beads away from her before she began to filter through them. They were of the body and its position. "There was an alligator on him? Was it responsible in some way?"

"No," Jason answered. "The alligator didn't have anything to do with him. Critter was there I think because of the smell of blood. The guy had a gash in his forehead and was just bleeding like a stuck pig. The gator I think had tried to pull him down, but he didn't have any luck. He did end up taking part of his hand with him though. Once he got a taste he wasn't leaving."

"Wow," Charlie said. "Please don't tell me that you killed him."

"Okay," Jason said. "I won't tell you. Naw, he disappeared before it came to that. It was kinda weird actually. Like he knew or something."

Charlie nodded and continued to flip through

several photographs until she saw the victim. A cold finger touched her heart.

"Oh my God," Charlie said. Her hand floated to her throat and touched the tender bruised skin of her neck. "Jason, this is the man who attacked me. Or his ghost attacked me I mean."

"Are you sure?"

"Positive."

"And his daughter asked you for a curse?"

"Yes," Charlie said, feeling sick to her stomach. "I don't know any witch that would use that sort of magic. Did you notice if there was a mark on his body?"

"No, I didn't see any kind of mark. Are you saying this thing leaves a mark?"

"Yeah, it does, but," Charlie ran her fingers through her hair. "I don't know if you could even see it."

"Can you see it?"

"Jason—" Charlie shook her head. "Please don't ask me to go look at this dead man's body. It's very possible his spirit is still hanging around."

"I would be there with you," he said.

"And what would you do? This guy seems to think I killed him."

"What about Tom?"

"What about Tom?" Charlie asked.

"Well isn't he a reaper? Couldn't he go with us

and do that thing he did to that ... You know—" Jason paused, a grimace on his face. He shuddered. "Never mind. That's probably not a good idea."

"No, it's not," Charlie said. She sighed and put her forehead on the table.

"Are you all right?" He reached across the table and touched her arm.

"Yeah, I'm fine. I'm just gathering the strength I'm gonna need that's all."

"I promise you I will not leave your side. And I will not let anything or anyone hurt you. Dead or alive."

Charlie shifted her gaze from the grimy linoleum floor to Jason's warm, hazel eyes.

"Well with that kind of promise who am I to say no?"

CHAPTER 5

C harlie had never been to the morgue before and she stuck close to Jason as they wound their way through the halls to the Medical Examiner's Office.

"Wait here," Jason said and approached a young man in scrubs. He flashed his badge, and they talked briefly. Charlie glanced around. She hated hospitals. There were always spirits lingering in the halls. The dead who for whatever reason never saw the light. She did her best to ignore the three spirits they passed on the way in but here in the morgue it was harder. The chill settled around her shoulders. She wasn't sure whether it was because they just naturally kept the department colder or if it was from the spirits standing in front of the wall of freezers staring at them, bewildered, as if they weren't sure exactly how they got there. Thankfully, she did not see the one spirit she was most afraid of. Tom had really chosen the wrong profession she thought, he probably would've had better odds catching spirits as a medical examiner. She would make sure to ask him why he chose a funeral director the next time she saw him. Jason gestured for her to come forward and she followed him and the young man over to the wall of freezers.

"This is Kyle," Jason said. "He's the medical examiner's assistant."

"Nice to meet you," she said. She offered up a weak smile, and he nodded and returned a smile of his own.

"I'm sorry for your loss ma'am," Kyle said. Charlie's eyes widened, and she glanced at Jason who made a face that said just play along.

"Thank you," Charlie said. "I appreciate that."

Kyle pulled on the handle of the freezer and the drawer rolled out. A thin, white plastic bag encased the corpse. It was not what she expected, having seen big, thick black bags on television. Kyle opened the bag and folded it back, so she could take a good look at the face inside. She didn't expect the smell that hit her and she immediately covered her mouth and nose with her hand.

"Sorry about that," Kyle said. "He was evidently in the elements for a couple of days."

"Right," Charlie said, choking out the word. Charlie looked down and immediately recognized the man she had faced off with in the parking lot just a few days ago. How had this happened to you? "Can you open the bag a little more?"

Kyle looked mildly surprised, but he nodded and did as she asked. A fresh Y-incision scarred the man's chest and torso but it didn't obscure the faint symbol glowing on the pale skin, centered over his heart.

"Would you mind if I had a moment alone with him?" She looked to Jason. Jason nodded and cast a glance at the ME's assistant.

Kyle shrugged his slim shoulders. "Sure. I'll be right over here, okay?"

"Thank you," she said. Jason continued to stand next to her, and she pinched her eyebrows together and glared at him.

"Oh, you want me to leave too?" he whispered.

"Yes," she whispered. "If I'm in for a penny I'm in for a pound. I certainly don't want Kyle to think I'm not the man's relative."

Jason nodded. He walked over to Kyle's desk and started to chat him up, distracting him from whatever Charlie's intentions were.

Charlie held her hand over the man's chest just above the mark and closed her eyes. She took a deep breath and tried to picture the maker of the curse. After a moment her mind drifted and a pair of hands appeared, carefully knotting a piece of what looked like silk or cotton floss. The hands were young and delicate with black-painted fingernails and several silver rings adorning her fingers. The ring on her left hand had a woven pentacle with either a black onyx or a black tourmaline stone in the center. Whoever she was, she identified as a witch. Female and young, a girl or young woman, though it was hard to tell which.

Charlie had felt her intentions as she added beads and knots to the string. Bone, feather and hair. Her intentions were cold and detached but seemed to Charlie to make the spell stronger. She would have to ask Evangeline about that. Since intention was as much an ingredient in a spell as any of the physical elements, how could being cold and dispassionate about the process reinforce the spell? Of course, maybe the girl was just a psychopath.

Charlie tried to change her view, but no matter what she did, she could only see the person's hands. Never her face. A small blue china bowl held the carved bone beads and a small white porcelain bowl held black and white clay beads with various designs on them. Some were intricately patterned with black flowers on white clay. Others were more abstract stripes and squares. Had the spell caster also made the beads? Was there any significance to them or did she just think they were pretty and suited her spell?

A hundred other questions went through Charlie's head as she watched the hands take several strands of hair and braid them with the string before continuing.

When the young woman finished, Charlie counted forty knots. Charlie racked her brain and tried to remember if the young woman that had hidden in her car was wearing nail polish. She didn't remember seeing any jewelry.

Another pair of hands entered the scene. An older pair of hands with long, bony fingers and painted red nails took the beads from the younger woman, inspecting them. Was the young witch her apprentice? The older woman's hands handed the beads back to the girl and went on to point a forefinger, shaking it as if she were scolding the younger witch. When the older woman walked away the young woman fisted her hand tightly around the beads before she threw them on the floor in anger.

A warm hand shook Charlie's shoulder, and she almost jumped out of her skin. Her eyes flew open and a little scream caught in her throat. She turned, holding her hand over her heart. "Oh my God, you scared the crap out of me," she scolded Jason.

"I'm sorry. I did call your name. But you didn't um ..." Jason lowered his voice, "seem to hear me."

Her cheeks flooded with heat and her gaze flitted

towards Kyle who was watching with awkward curiosity. "Oh. Sorry. I was concentrating."

"Yeah, I figured. Did you find what you were looking for?"

Charlie cleared her throat and nodded. "Thank you, deputy, yes I did. I would like to leave now."

"Yeah, I think that be a good idea," Jason said under his breath. He turned and waved at Kyle. "Thanks, man."

"Yes, sure. Anytime." Kyle held up his hand and waved.

Jason led Charlie out by the elbow. Once they were safely in the hall, he stopped and stared at her expectantly.

"What did you see?"

"We're definitely dealing with a witch. But it was —" she stopped, not sure exactly what she had seen.

"It was what?"

"I think there may be two of them."

"Well that's just great. Did you see their faces?"

"No. All I saw were their hands."

"Their hands?" Jason said.

"Yep. A young pair and an older pair. Both female. I think the woman with the younger hands is apprenticing with the woman with the older hands."

"Okay." Jason scrubbed his chin. "I got a look at the preliminary autopsy report for the guy. There's thinking he died accidentally from the head wound he sustained. We found his boat not far from where we found his body and there was a big old pool of blood. He had a blood alcohol level of .1 and they didn't find any poisons or drugs in his system, but of course it will be weeks before they get all the tests back so that could change. Right now, all I have is a drunk guy who slipped and fell and hit his head, which is a tragedy but not a crime."

"Jason, someone cursed him. Could it have looked like an accident? Hell, yes, but that doesn't change the fact that somebody wanted him dead."

"Charlie, unless I have a suspicious death on the report from the medical examiner, I don't have reason to investigate it as a crime. And nothing at the scene suggests this was a crime other than those beads. For all I know the dude liked jewelry. Is it weird? Sure, but it's not something I can continue investigating."

"So that's it?"

"Yeah, I'm afraid it is. Your witch did a damn good job at covering it up as an accident."

"There has to be something that can be done," Charlie said.

"Maybe there is but I can't do it. I'm sorry."

"What if I do it?"

Jason sighed and stepped closer to her. "If you do, I don't want to know anything about it. Especially if it involves anything illegal. Do you understand?"

"Yeah, I understand. Can you at least tell me his name?"

Jason shook his head. "Nope. Sorry. But if you pay attention to Channel 5 news, there will probably be a story on it."

"Okay. Well that's something I guess."

"Come on. I'll take you back."

Charlie nodded and followed him out to the car. Somehow, she would have to find the witch and her apprentice and stop them from ever cursing anyone again.

CHAPTER 6

The AC in her truck was broken, and both windows were down funneling warm sticky air through the cab. Jen hung her arm out letting her hand catch the currents in waves and Ruby copied her mother, sticking her little hand out of the passenger side window, trailing it up and down. They passed Henninger's strawberry farm, which was closed for the season now and the dark, freshly plowed field gave way to pine trees.

The blacktop out here turned a dusky gray and only the faintest of a yellow line hinted at a division between the right side and the left. There were no houses or developments and most of the woods were boggy, so when she saw the silver Volvo on the side of the road Jen slowed down. The driver was slumped over the wheel, but Jen recognized the car. It belonged to Debra Duguid, the mayor's wife and Kristin Duguid's mother. Jen pulled her truck over in front of the car.

"Baby, you stay here in the truck. You understand me? Don't get out unless I tell you to."

"Yes, Mama." Ruby nodded, her little face etched with worry.

Jen dug through her messenger bag and grabbed her cell phone. The hairs on the back of her neck prickled a warning as she walked to the car. She bent down and knocked on the window. It was late April, still spring by the calendar, but the afternoons had already started to reach the high eighties. The inside of that car would be like an oven. Jen tried the door handle, and it gave easily.

"Debra," Jen said as she opened the car door wide. "Oh god Debra," Jen muttered as the heat from the car slapped her in the face. She touched Debra's back. The old woman was burning up. Jen tried to push her back to a reclining position, but Debra jerked away. The old woman turned her head. Her cloudy gray eyes fixed on Jen and she gurgled, foam dripping from the corners of her mouth.

She heard Ruby cry, "Mommy!"

Jen glanced down and found Ruby right behind her. "Ruby Ellen, go back to the truck."

"But Mommy," Ruby cried. "I'm scared."

"I know you are Baby, but I need you to go to the truck so I can help Miss Debra,"

"What's wrong with her?" Ruby asked, not taking her eyes off the old woman.

"I don't know, honey. Please go back to the truck."

Ruby scrunched up her face but did as she was told.

"Debra!" Jen knelt next to the woman. Debra's pale crepe-y skin was damp with sweat and her eyes rolled back into her head revealing only the whites. Jen's heart leapt into her throat. She fumbled with the phone in her pocket, dialing 911 as she pressed her free hand against Debra's neck trying to find a pulse.

"911, what's your emergency?" the operator asked.

"I have a woman, Debra Duguid. She's collapsed in her car—"

Jen's mouth went dry as she spoke. Her eyes settled on Debra's chest. Was it moving? She couldn't tell. "She's unconscious."

"What's your location?"

"I'm about two miles north of Henninger's strawberry farm. On Old Pointe Road."

"Is she breathing?" the operator asked.

"I don't know. I can't tell—" Jen's managed a whisper. "Please hurry."

"I have an officer about five minutes away. I need you to just stay on the line with me."

"All right." Jen took the old woman's hand in hers. A moan escaped Debra's mouth.

"Oh, thank you, God," Jen muttered, relief flooding through her. "Debra, you're going to be okay. Help's coming."

She leaned in close and stroked the coarse gray hair off Debra's forehead. Her eyes scanned over Debra's chest, trying to figure out if the woman had been injured or if there was some other apparent reason for her illness.

A siren announced the arrival of the ambulance and the sheriff before their lights did.

"They're here," she told the operator and hung up the phone. She stood up waving her arms over her head. The two vehicles pulled around them, parking on the grassy shoulder. Two EMT's jumped out of the ambulance with their bags and Jen stepped back. They wore latex gloves, but Jen watched them as they went about their work of taking Debra Duguid. She silently said a quick protection blessing. Without knowing the cause of Debra's unconsciousness, it was all she could offer for now.

"Hey, Jen," the deputy said as he approached her.

Jen turned her head and found Billy Eisener approaching. "Hey, Billy. We go months without seeing each other and bam, twice in one week."

She'd known Billy almost her entire life. He was a year older than her and he and Lisa had dated off and on for almost seven years. Seeing his Basset Hound-like eyes filled with concern comforted her.

"Yeah I know, weird, huh?" He pulled a pen and a small notepad from his front breast pocket. "Can you tell me what happened here?"

"I don't know. Something bad I think. I was driving Ruby home from school and we came across Debra slumped over in her car. The door was closed, and I stopped to see if I could help. She's in bad shape. I have no idea how long she's been sitting out in this heat."

"Uh huh." Billy's face stayed serious. "Yeah, it's a hot one today. Then what happened?"

"I opened the car door and found her foaming at the mouth, unconscious. That's when I called 911."

They both watched as the EMTs lifted Debra onto a gurney. "Is she going to be all right?"

The EMT with short blond hair nodded, his squinty blue eyes solemn. He barely looked a day over eighteen. "We're gonna do everything we can, ma'am."

"Where are y'all taking her?" Jen asked. Debra's pale skin had taken on a grayish tint, and some part of her knew the EMT was just telling her what she wanted to hear.

The EMT climbed inside the ambulance, glancing back over his shoulder. He threw out the words, "St. Francis." He yanked the door shut behind him and the lights and siren came on at almost the same time.

"Someone should call Kristen and let her know what's happened." Jen glanced down at her phone, thumbing through her contacts for the pharmacy's number. "And the mayor, too, I guess."

"Don't you worry about it, Jen," Billy said, reassuring her. "I can take care of getting in touch with her family."

"I just saw Kristen the other day. She came into the cafe for a pie," Jen mused.

"Uh huh," he said, still scribbling in his notebook. "You'll be around if I have more questions, right?"

"Of course."

"All right." He pulled a card from his pocket and shoved it into her hand. "You think of anything else you give me a call, all right?"

"I will." Jen nodded, looking down at the card. It was funny that he gave it to her. She knew exactly where to find him. "Thanks, Billy."

"It's good to see you, Jen, even if the circumstances aren't all that great."

"You, too."

"Tell Lisa I said hi." He gave her a smile as he walked back to his cruiser.

"Tell her yourself," Jen quipped, breathing a little easier now that the crisis was in someone else's hands.

"I would, but she doesn't return my calls anymore." He sighed. "She's the only woman I know to get mad at a marriage proposal."

Jen's eyes widened and an awkward smile curved her lips. "She is a conundrum sometimes."

A shadow crossed his face, and he tipped his hat. "Well, I'll see you around, Jen."

"Yeah. See ya, Billy." She waved and climbed into the cab of her truck. Billy got into his cruiser, flipped his lights on and made a U-turn, heading in the direction of the ambulance.

Ruby launched herself into her mother's arms.

"Oh, sweetie," Jen soothed. "I'm so sorry you were scared. But I had to help that Miss Debra. Are you okay?"

"I'm okay. Is that lady okay?" Ruby asked, her voice quivering.

Jen sighed, hugging her daughter close. "I sure hope so, honey."

She kissed Ruby on the top of the head and strapped her back into her seat. Jen pulled her phone from her pocket and found the contact she was looking for and pressed the call icon on her phone as she put the truck in gear, pulled off the shoulder and made a U-turn heading back toward town.

"Hi Kristen, It's Jen Holloway. I'm so sorry to have to tell you this but ..."

* * *

BEFORE JEN COULD FINISH EXPLAINING EVERYTHING Kristen had broken down into tears and Jen knew there was no way her friend would be able to drive safely all the way into Charleston. So Jen made a quick call to her father, asking him to swing by The Kitchen Witch to pick up Ruby. He didn't ask many questions and for that she was grateful. And as usual Evangeline was happy to watch Ruby until her father arrived.

Evangeline took her great niece's hand in hers and led her to the end of the counter. She pulled out her special basket of coloring books and crayons that she kept just for times like these and put Ruby to work "making signs" for the cafe.

"Go on now." Evangeline shooed Jen out of the cafe. "Go take care of your friend. I'll take care of this little one till her granddaddy gets here." It was moments like these Jen knew she'd made the right decision to come home and raise Ruby instead of trying to do it all by herself in San Francisco.

Thirty minutes later Jen pulled her old truck into the parking lot at St. Francis Hospital with Kristen in tow. By the time they arrived it was too late. Debra Duguid had been announced dead on arrival. Kristen shattered into a million little pieces and all Jen could do was wrap her arms around her friend and wait for the first ebb in the wave of grief to take Kristen home. There were people to call and plans to make, but Jen convinced Kristen that all that could wait until tomorrow. The only person Kristen insisted on calling before leaving was her father. When he didn't answer his phone, Kristen left a message that both shocked and intrigued Jen.

"Since you're not answering your phone, Daddy, you leave me no choice but to inform you that your wife of thirty-five years is on her way to the morgue. Are you happy now?" Spittle wet Kristen's lips and the screen of her smart phone as she said the bitter words. "You'd better prepare yourself. Cause when the paper finds out that you couldn't even be bothered to pick up the phone to get the news they're gonna want to know why and you know what? I'm gonna tell 'em."

She pressed the little red phone icon on the screen of her smart phone, ending the call before the tears overwhelmed her again. "I'm sorry you had to hear that," Kristen said softly.

"That's okay." Jen shook her head and called up a sympathetic smile. "No worries. It's none of my business."

"He's having an affair you know," Kristen said. Her face contorted with pain and disgust.

"No, I—I," Jen stammered. What was she supposed to do with that little gem? She tucked it away inside her head for later evaluation. "I didn't."

"Well, he is," Kristen said matter-of-factly, then she cursed him under her breath.

"Come on honey, let's get you home. I think you've had enough for today."

"I should call my brother." Kristen wiped the heel of her hand across her cheek, swiping away errant tears.

"You can call him on the way back." Jen rubbed the top of Kristen's arm, trying to comfort her. Kristen nodded, grief molding her face into a grimace.

Jen led her out of the hospital and got her into the truck. The trip home was going to take longer than the trip into Charleston from the looks of it and as she pulled into the late afternoon traffic, Jen wished the radio worked.

For nearly twenty minutes Kristen stared straight ahead saying nothing. Her glassy blue eyes barely blinked and every once in a while, her bottom lip would quiver and Jen thought a fresh onslaught of tears might start but it didn't. When Kristen's purse began to buzz, she didn't seem to notice it.

"Kristen? I think your phone is ringing," Jen said. "Maybe it's your daddy calling you back."

Kristen nodded and grabbed her over-sized Coach bag, digging through the contents — pulling out a wallet, a notebook, several pens, some loose hard candies and a couple of different prescription bottles. She laid them on the seat next to her.

Jen glanced down. She didn't mean to be nosy, but she couldn't help herself. One of the prescription bottles stared at her — clearly longing to be read: Joshua Helms. Lorazepam. 2mg. Take 1 tablet twice a day. Someone honked a horn behind Jen, making her jump, bringing her attention back to the road. Finally, Kristen found her phone.

"Hey," Kristen said, softly. She gave Jen a sideways glance and turned her head toward the window. "No. We're on our way back home now." Kristen kept her voice just above a whisper and her answers short. It reminded Jen of the way her sister Lisa used to talk to Billy on the phone — like she didn't want anyone to know she was talking to him. "Uh-huh. Yes." Kristen sniffled, and her tone grew squeakier, as if it was painful to say the words. "Yes. I know, I can't believe it either. Thank you. I'll see you soon." Kristen disconnected and cleared her throat. "That was, uh. That was a good friend of mine. Just checking on me to see how I am."

"You don't have to explain," Jen said. "I'm glad you have somebody you can count on."

"Me, too." Kristen stared at the screen of her phone for a few seconds before her shoulders slumped. "I don't know what to do next, Jen. What should I do next?"

"Oh sweetie, I know this is hard. But you and your dad and your brother will have to make some decisions together. Hopefully your mom and dad had some sort of plan in place."

"Yeah, I'm sure they did."

A few minutes later Jen pulled into the parking lot of Duguid's Pharmacy and Kristen gathered her things off the seat, shoving them back into her purse.

"Are you sure don't want to come to my house tonight?" Jen asked. "We've got plenty of room."

"No, I just want to go home." Kristen opened the door. "You're sweet to offer though."

Jen nodded. "Well, you call me if you need anything. Okay?"

Kristen managed a weak smile. "I will. Thank you. Really Jen, for everything. You're a good friend."

Jen placed her hand over Kristen's and gave it a squeeze before Kristen slid out of the truck and hurried toward her Toyota Camry.

"Joshua Helms," Jen said aloud. "What's your prescription doing in Kristen Duguid's purse?" Jen waited for Kristen to start her car before pulling away and heading toward home.

CHAPTER 7

The sun sank low in the sky and Jen was glad for the longer spring days. She pulled into the long driveway leading to her father's house, the wheels crunching on the gravel. Music drifted across the yard as she approached the house, making her smile. The driveway stretched along the side of the house, curving around to a large covered parking pad, where a twenty-year-old Mercedes diesel was parked. Behind this car was a twenty-five-year-old Ford pickup. The Mercedes was her father's. A leftover status symbol from his days as a cardiologist. The pickup was Evangeline's. Jen parked her old truck next to Evangeline's and hopped out. The humid evening air had started to cool and goose bumps broke out along her arms.

Her father raised his hand to wave from his seat on the porch swing. Ruby's little hand shot up, too. Jen returned their waves and tromped up the steps to the rambling, low country-style house. The white clapboard had benefited from a fresh coat of paint in March and it glowed eerily as twilight descended.

"Well hey, y'all," Jen said. Ruby sat on the swing next to her grandfather, her long dark wavy hair glistened with wetness and she wore a pair of pink striped pajama bottoms and a pink T-shirt. A large book lay across her lap.

"Hey mama," Ruby chirped. "I'm reading to granddaddy."

"I see that. Did you get the rest of your homework done?"

"Yes ma'am," Ruby said.

"Did you eat?" her father asked. Inside the house, the sound of water running drifted through the screen door, followed by the clang of dishes.

"No," Jen said. "Where's Lisa?"

"She called and said she'd be late."

"Is Charlie here?" Jen looked across the wide yard to the small cottage near the edge of the property where her cousin lived. She could see a faint light in the kitchen.

"She's inside," Jack said.

Jen cocked her head listening to the sound of

dishes being put into the drainer. "You're just letting her do the dishes aren't you?"

He shrugged, a grin playing at the corner of his mouth. "She doesn't like the way I do them."

Jen sighed and crossed her arms, shaking her head. "She doesn't live here. You are a bad host."

"What?" he shrugged. "She wouldn't have it any other way."

"Right," Jen chuckled.

"Now don't go giving him a hard time," Evangeline said through the screen door. In her hands were a blue willow dish and a red gingham tea towel. She rubbed the dish dry. "Jack and I have a system worked out, and Charlie's helping."

Jen folded her arms across her chest and snorted. "Oh yeah, he's got a system all right. You could sell that you know," Jen said. "How to keep a clean house and never do a lick of housework by Jack Holloway. It'd sell a million copies. You'd be stinking rich."

"Yep," Jack grinned. "And I'd cut every single one of you out of my will."

"Even me, Granddaddy?" Ruby batted her innocent blue eyes at him.

"Oh, no baby girl, I'd never cut you out of my will." He kissed his granddaughter on top of the head and Jen rolled her eyes.

"I've saved you supper," Evangeline said. A pair

of headlights flashed across the yard and a white BMW pulled into the driveway, parking behind Jen's old truck. Lisa Holloway exited her car, staring up at the porch.

"Well, I wasn't expecting a reception," Lisa said, reaching for the bobby pins holding her strawberry blond hair in a tight bun at the nape of her neck. She shook out her long locks, running her fingers through it as she climbed the steps.

"Am I too late for supper?" Lisa asked, putting her hands on her slender hips.

"Nope." Evangeline pulled open the screen door. "Come on in and I'll heat it up for you. You too, Jen."

"Fifteen minutes more of reading Ruby. It's almost time to start getting ready for bed," Jen said.

"Awww ..." Ruby sat back hard against the porch swing and stuck her lip out.

"I'll make sure she comes inside." Jack swung his arm across the back of the swing protectively. Jen gave her father a pointed look. He knew better than to get involved with her parenting.

Her stomach growled, and she narrowed her eyes. "Fifteen minutes," she said and went into the house before her father could make a smart remark.

Inside, the air was warm and the delicious aroma of shrimp and grits permeated the kitchen.

"How long have you been here?" Jen asked Evangeline, pulling two clean plates from the cabinet. Her eyes went to the clean plates and pans in the dish drainer. A stack of round grit cakes were on a plate next to the stove and her mother's old cast iron pan was sitting on the burner waiting to be used. Another pot was on the back burner with its lid clamped tightly in place. The familiar click, click, click echoed through the space before a whoosh of flame appeared beneath the well-seasoned frying pan. Evangeline had already pulled out the jar of bacon grease from the refrigerator and scooped a couple of teaspoons onto the heating metal.

"Mmm this looks good. What's the occasion?" Jen moved closer, evaluating the rounds. She held the plate to her face and took a sniff.

"No occasion, I just thought it'd be nice for a change," Evangeline said, relieving Jen of the plate. With a metal spatula she lifted the first cake and set it into slick grease. It sizzled, making Jen's mouth water.

"You know I've been thinking about playing with this recipe for the cafe," Jen said. "Maybe we could chop the shrimp into the grits along with a little green onion, fry them and serve them drizzled with gravy."

"That sounds good, but I want more than just a drizzle of gravy," Lisa said crowding in next to her sister. Evangeline flipped the grit cake, revealing a golden crust.

Charlie finished washing up the last of the dishes from the first sitting and threw the dishtowel over her shoulder. "What happened with Debra?"

Jen took a breath and blew it out. "She passed."

"Oh my stars, that's awful," Charlie said.

"What?" Evangeline's head turned sharply, her blue eyes boring into Jen. "I just saw her yesterday. How did that happen?"

"I don't know," Jen said, shaking her head. She folded her arms across her chest. "They think she may have had some sort of stroke or seizure. I guess they'll have to do an autopsy to find out for sure."

"Well, I was never a big fan of hers, but I'm still sorry to hear it. How's Kristin taking it?" Evangeline asked, gently lifting the edge of grit cake to check for color.

Jen shrugged her shoulder. "Kristin will be all right I think. I mean she was a mess, of course, but she left a voice mail chewing out her daddy for not being there, so she'll be fine. I saw Billy Eisener for the second time this week." Jen gave her sister a pointed look.

Lisa returned a bored look. "So?"

"So he said to tell you hi," Jen teased. "What's going on there?"

"Nothing." Lisa folded her arms across her chest,

ignoring her sister's look of doubt. "Is supper almost ready, Evangeline?"

"Yes, y'all go on to the table," Evangeline ordered, scooping the cakes onto a clean plate. For a minute, Jen felt like she was eight years old again, when her aunt had lived with them and took care of them. "I'll bring your food when it's done."

Jen nudged Lisa's elbow and took a seat at the planked table in the center of the kitchen. Lisa pulled a box of cheese crackers from the cabinet, sat next to her sister and began to nibble. Charlie pulled a chocolate pie from the refrigerator and cut a piece for herself.

"Where's Daphne?" Lisa asked.

"She had a late appointment and didn't want to come all the way out here." Evangeline carried two steaming hot plates and put one in front of Jen. The smell of shrimp in savory gravy made Jen's mouth water.

"This looks delicious," Lisa said.

"Anybody else want a piece of pie?" Charlie asked.

"I'm good, sweetie," Evangeline said, picking up the heavy iron pan to clean it. Jen and Lisa both had their mouths full, but shook their heads no. Charlie put the pie back into the refrigerator and took a seat at the table across from Jen and Lisa.

A few minutes later Jack Holloway carried his

granddaughter piggy-back into the house. He bent down close to Jen, grunting a little. "Give your mama a kiss good night," he said. Ruby pecked her lips against Jen's cheek.

"I can take her, Daddy," Jen said.

"Nah, you go ahead and eat your supper. I'll tuck her in," he said.

"All right, then," Jen said, giving Ruby a quick kiss. "I'll be up in a minute to say good night. Have you brushed your teeth?"

"Yes'm," Ruby nodded. Jack straightened up and Ruby grabbed onto his neck.

"Good girl. Say goodnight everybody," Jen instructed.

Ruby waved. "Good night."

"Good night, sweetie," Lisa said, before taking a bite of her shrimp and grits.

"Night, Ruby," Charlie said.

"Good night, baby girl." Evangeline sidled up next to Jack and kissed Ruby on the cheek. "Sweet dreams."

"Thank you, Daddy." Jen watched as her father trudged up the steps to the second floor, waiting until he was out of earshot to continue their earlier conversation.

"I know this is going to sound crazy," Jen said, taking the side of her fork and slicing through a generously sized shrimp. "But I think Kristen may be having an affair with ..."

She scooped some grit cake and gravy onto her fork and pierced the piece of shrimp before shoving it into her mouth.

Lisa mumbled something with her mouth half full of food. Evangeline crossed her arms and sat down in the empty chair next to Charlie.

"With who?" Charlie asked.

"Josh Helms."

"Oh my gosh, really?" Charlie sliced into her pie and took a bite.

"Josh and Melinda are separated. I don't think you can actually call it an affair," Lisa said matter-of-factly.

"How do you know they're separated?" Jen asked.

"Josh filed the papers with one of my partners. I saw him in the office just this week," Lisa said taking another bite.

"Well, there you go," Evangeline said. Her long silver hair hung to her shoulders, and a halo of frizz from the humidity glowed pale white in the incandescent light.

"Well that almost makes me feel sorry for Melinda Helms," Jen said.

"Almost," Lisa chuckled. "Bless her cold calculating heart."

"Well I feel sorry for Kristen," Charlie said. "Losing her mama all of a sudden like that. Are you going to the funeral?"

Jen paused with her fork in midair. "Yeah. I think I should. I think we all should. What do you think?"

"I think Kristen is your friend, not mine. I mean I feel bad for her but I don't want to go to a funeral." Lisa pushed a piece of shrimp around on her plate.

"I'll go with you Jen," Charlie said.

"Wonderful. Thank you, Charlie." Jen smiled.

"You are welcome." Charlie smiled and then took another bite of her pie.

"Kiss ass," Lisa muttered under her breath.

"All right now," Evangeline scolded.

"That reminds me." Jen narrowed her eyes, and an evil smiled tugged at her lips. "Billy Eisener asked you to marry him?"

Charlie paused mid-chew and shifted her gaze to the exchange between her cousins.

Lisa's face lost some of its color and she glared at her sister. "He told you that?"

"Yep. Said you got mad," Jen said.

Charlie shifted her plate out of the way, folded her arms and leaned forward on the table, staring at Lisa intently.

Lisa's lips curved down at the corners. "I swear to god, he has the biggest mouth."

"Is that why y'all broke up?" Charlie asked.

"Yes," Lisa said her tone curt.

"You didn't even tell us he asked," Jen said sounding a little wounded.

Lisa put her fork down and it clanked against the side of the plate. "Why would I? It's not like I was ever gonna marry him."

"What happens if Jason asks? When you break his heart, you gonna keep that from us too?" Charlie asked, her face a stone mask.

"What?" Lisa almost choked on the word.

"What are you talking about, Charlie?" Jen felt the line between her eyes deepen as she stared at her cousin.

"Lisa knows what I'm talking about, don't you?" Charlie locked her gaze on Lisa's shocked face. Jen watched with awe and confusion as her sister and cousin seemed to engage in some unspoken conversation. Finally Charlie spoke again.

"He is my friend and my partner. Whatever you do, don't hurt him."

Lisa's cheeks reddened. She opened her mouth to speak but Charlie held her hand up, cutting her off. "You know what? I don't want to hear it. Not after the week I've had." Charlie scraped her chair across the old wood floor of the kitchen and rose to her feet. "Thank you for dinner, Evangeline, it was delicious."

Charlie gave Jen a weary smile. "I'll call you tomorrow, Jen."

"Oh ... okay," Jen stammered. She watched as Charlie walked out of the kitchen, letting the screen door slam behind her. Jen and Evangeline both shifted their attention to Lisa.

"Are you dating Jason?" Jen finally asked.

Lisa gritted her teeth and gave her sister an angry look. "No. I am not dating him."

"Well Charlie's certainly got a bee in her bonnet about him," Evangeline said.

Jen stared into her sister's green eyes. "Are you sleeping with him?" she mouthed.

Lisa scowled. "That is none of y'alls business."

"What's none of our business?" Jack said as he entered the kitchen.

"Nothing, Daddy." Lisa folded her napkin and put it on the table next to her plate. "It doesn't matter. I think I've had enough. Thank you, Evangeline, dinner was lovely. I better be getting home now."

"Don't go away mad," Jen said. "Talk to me."

"What's going on?" Jack said, moving so he could look at his daughters. "What're y'all fighting about?"

"We're not fighting," Lisa said. She squirmed for a moment then picked up her fork again and took another bite of food. Jen waited, knowing that eventually her sister would talk about it.

"Well, if you were dating him, which I know you

said you're not, if you were, I think it would be wonderful." Jen scooped another bite of food.

"Well, I'm glad you think so," Lisa said, her tone shifting from serious to wry. She dug into dinner again. "Since it is all about you."

"Oh my God, you totally are dating him," Jen teased.

"Shut up. I am not. It's just a fling, and he knows it. Charlie doesn't have to worry. Nobody's getting hurt."

Jen laughed gleefully. Lisa opened up like a clam sometimes — a little at a time when the water was just right. Then she would slam shut with very little provocation.

"What are they talking about?" Jack looked to Evangeline.

Evangeline rose from the table, shaking her head, a smile on her face. "Boys." She chuckled. "Some things never change. Do they Jack?"

"No, I guess they don't. You're being safe, right?" Jack said directing the question to Lisa.

"What?" Lisa gave her father a confused look.

"You know, when you have sex," Jack said dryly.

"Daddy!" Jen and Lisa said in a chorus.

"What? I'm a doctor. It's not like I don't know that my grown daughters have sex. I just want to make sure you're being safe about it."

"Oh my God." Lisa rubbed her forehead with one hand. "Just kill me now."

Jen laughed again, this time from her belly. Lisa pushed away from the table and stood up.

"Aw, don't run off just because Dad's nosy," Jen said.

"Nah, it's not that. I gotta go. I still have some work to finish." Lisa leaned in and kissed her father on his bearded cheek. "Good night. Evangeline, dinner was delicious thank you."

"You are most welcome, sweetheart," Evangeline said, giving her a weary smile.

"Please go with me to Debra's funeral?" Jen asked.

Lisa made a disgusted noise in the back of her throat. "Charlie said she'd go with you." Lisa slung her purse strap onto her shoulder.

"I know but ... I want you there."

"Why?"

"I just do. Please?"

Lisa rolled her eyes. "Fine, just let me know when it is and I'll take a couple of hours off."

"Thank you," Jen said. Lisa gave them all one last wave before heading out.

Evangeline sighed. "Well, I should be going, too. I'm opening tomorrow." She stood and stretched her back. "I'll bid y'all good night."

"Good night," Jen said. "And thank you for taking care of Ruby today."

Evangeline squeezed Jen's shoulder. "Anytime."

"Night 'Vange." Jack grinned. "Thanks for cookin' *and* cleanin'."

Evangeline chuckled, gathering her things before disappearing into the quiet of the night.

CHAPTER 8

Jen was refilling the tea at table seven when Ben Sutton walked into the restaurant. He glanced around as if he was looking for her and when he spotted her a smile stretched across his face. Her heart fluttered a little.

"Hey, you're spilling my tea," the woman at table seven said.

Jen looked down at the mess she had made by overfilling the glass. "Oh my gosh, I am so sorry. Let me just get you a fresh glass. I apologize."

Jen's cheeks heated, and she took the tea glass and dumped it in the sink behind the counter. She took a fresh glass and filled it with iced tea.

"Hey Dottie," she said to the older woman at the end of the counter refilling the ketchups. "Can you take this to table seven for me please and I spilled some tea on the floor. If you wouldn't mind mopping it up, I'd really appreciate it."

"Sure thing, Jen," Dottie said, taking the tea glass.

Ben approached the counter and took a seat.

"You're back," Jen said.

"I am." He smiled and folded his hands on the counter.

"Did you find a place to live?" she asked.

"No, I'm still looking," he said. "I still live out of the hotel. But hopefully I'll be able to find something soon."

"Well, that will be wonderful, for you. I mean," she said. Her face felt downright hot.

"It will be wonderful. As you say." He smiled again.

"What can I get for you today?" she said, taking her order pad from the front pocket of her apron.

"What would you suggest?" he asked, never taking his blue eyes off of her.

"Well how adventurous are you feeling?"

"I am always up for an adventure," he said. He leaned forward on his elbows. She liked the way he looked at her. It had been a long time since anyone had looked at her that way.

"Well, I have a soft shell crab sandwich with a spicy sauce and homemade onion rings that is pretty delicious if I do say so myself."

"I'm game," he said. "

"Would you like iced tea to drink?"

That would be wonderful."

Jen wrote his order down on the ticket then slipped it on the order wheel and turned it toward the kitchen. "Order up."

The swinging kitchen door opened and Evangeline emerged. She had her purse strap slung over her shoulder. "All right Jen, I am off. Manuel's in the back and he is going to finish up your order for you."

"Thank you," she said. "Everything has been delicious today."

"I thought you were the chef," Ben said.

"Not the only one," Jen said with a shy laugh. "Evangeline here makes award-winning food. If you come back on Saturday make sure you order the pork chop special. It is delectable. There's no other word for it."

Evangeline leaned in and touched her arm to Jen's. "She's just being sweet. Enjoy your food." Evangeline walked around the counter and left for the day.

"So I was wondering," Ben said, taking a sip of his iced tea." "What is there to do in this town?"

"Well there are restaurants and there's the beach and there's the river. There's plenty to do," Jen said.

"What about a date? What is there to do on a date?" He settled his gaze on her and Jen felt like a deer staring into headlights on the highway.

"Well, I guess you could have dinner and go for ice cream or you could take a walk on the beach at sunset. During the summer there are concerts down on the pier."

"All that sounds really nice," he said softly. "Any chance I could get you to accompany me on one of those outings?"

"Me?" Jen said.

"Yeah, you," he grinned. "How about it? Are you up for it?"

"You should know I have a six-year-old daughter," she blurted out.

"Really? That's ... that's wonderful. I'd love to meet her sometime."

"Okay," she said, her voice a little squeaky.

"Okay," he said nodding. "It's a date."

"It's a date." Jen grinned. One of the customers signaled that they needed her attention and Jen floated away, her stomach flip-flopping with glee.

* * *

THE NEXT DAY CHARLIE STOOD OUTSIDE HER AUNT'S front door posing with her hand as if she were about to knock. But something kept stopping her.

It startled her when the door opened, and Evangeline stood there with a quizzical look on her face.

"How long you going to stand out here?" Evangeline said.

"Until I decide to knock?" Charlie said

Evangeline rolled her eyes and shook her head. "Come on girl, why don't you struggle with whatever is bothering you inside." She jerked her thumb towards her living room and glanced around. "That way the neighbors won't talk."

"Yes ma'am," Charlie said and followed Evangeline into the tidy living room of her condo. Family photos filled the spaces on the walls and tables. Charlie took a seat in one of the comfortable floral chairs near the pale blue denim couch. Evangeline sat on the couch, leaning forward with her elbows on her knees. Her silver hair hung over the front of one shoulder in a long braid that nearly reached her abdomen.

Evangeline focused her intense blue eyes on Charlie. "Now what's going on?"

"First, I'm really sorry about the dust up the other day at dinner. I didn't mean to go off on Lisa like that. Just something rubbed me wrong when she was talking about Billy."

"Honey, I appreciate that, but I'm not the one you need to apologize to," Evangeline said.

Charlie leaned her head back and closed her eyes. "I know."

"Now, what's really going on? There's something else that's been bugging you. I can feel it."

Charlie crossed her arms and hugged them to herself tightly. "Jason found the man who attacked me."

"Well that's great honey. Although I thought it was a ghost that attacked you."

"It was," Charlie said. "It was the ghost of a man that was walking through the Walmart parking lot last Saturday. He was angry and according to his stepdaughter a little drunk. I caught him looking into my car."

"I don't think I understand, sweetie. Are you saying that you knew the man?"

"I think *know* is a very strong word. I met him briefly in a parking lot last Saturday. And then he ended up dead in Seward's Nature Preserve. Killed by his own boat and stupidity I guess."

"Well stars above, why did he think *you* killed him then?"

"That I don't know exactly. What I do know is that he was cursed. By a witch's ladder."

Charlie peered into her aunt's face. Evangeline looked as if she had been slapped.

"Are you sure?"

"Yes, ma'am," Charlie said. "As sure as I'm sitting here. The problem is I don't know what to do. I don't know any witch capable of doing this, but I had a vision about her. Actually, there were two of them I think. A witch and her apprentice." Charlie leaned forward. "I was hoping that maybe you could give me some guidance."

"All right," Evangeline said in a measured way. "There's nothing inherently illegal about the witch's ladder itself. It's only when it's used as a death spell that it gets into dark magic territory. I guess I could contact the Council. See what they have to say."

"Well, Jason said he can't really help me because the man died from a head injury. The coroner deemed it an accidental death. His hands are tied."

"Well that may not be a bad thing. It's not like he's a witch and can protect himself."

"I know." Charlie tilted her head toward the window, pondering Evangeline's practical assessment. "I do think we need to find this witch. Before she hurts someone else."

"I agree." Evangeline got to her feet. "Wait here just a minute."

Charlie watched as her aunt disappeared down the short hallway that led to her bedroom. A few minutes later Evangeline returned with her cell phone. She searched through her contacts and found the name she was looking for and pressed the call button.

"Hi, Eileen," Evangeline said in a calm, serene voice. "This is Evangeline Ferebee. Yes, thank you,

I'm doing very well. I have a little problem. It looks like we may have a rogue witch situation here. Well, we know that there has been at least one death spell."

Charlie watched as her aunt nodded her head and made sounds of agreement into the phone.

"Okay, then. I appreciate the information. Oh, yes, we'll be careful." Evangeline nodded. "Thank you so much. Yes, you have a wonderful day yourself."

Evangeline pressed the red icon on her phone and turned to face her niece.

"Well?" Charlie asked. "Are they going to help us?"

"She gave me the number for the Defenders of Light."

"Who are the Defenders of Light?" Charlie asked.

"They are basically magical law enforcement," Evangeline said.

Charlie scooted up on the edge of her seat, a little excited at the thought. "I didn't even realize that we had magical law enforcement. I thought it was up to the local witch community to keep that sort of thing in line."

"Not when it comes to illegal spells, honey. Death spells. Torture spells. Those are sort of like the controlled substances of the magical world," Evangeline said. "And are highly regulated. Most people don't even have a death spell in their family's grimoire."

"Okay," Charlie said. "Let's call them. So they can come down and help us."

"You're awfully excited about this," Evangeline said. "Should I be worried?"

"No, absolutely not. It's great. It means I have somebody that I can count on."

"All right," Evangeline smiled. "I just don't want you to be disappointed if it doesn't turn out to be as exciting as working with Jason. That's all. A lot of these officers, well they tend to be solitary. I don't really think they work with a partner."

"Well, we'll just have to see about that, won't we?" Charlie said. "Now how do we contact them?"

CHAPTER 9

The bell rang, and teenagers flooded out of the classrooms. Charlie stood in the middle of a long hallway. She recognized the place immediately although it had been over 15 years since she'd been here. It was her old high school. Everything looked almost the same except the kids. The kids, while they looked like her kid. Only a little older. Charlie caught sight of the girl from her car, Ryan, and she followed her into a classroom.

This is a dream, Charlie thought.

Ryan sank down into the chair of the first desk in the row of desks running along the wall. Charlie glanced around taking it all in. A teacher walked through her and it shocked Charlie.

Charlie understood she was here for a reason. She took a deep breath and pushed her way into the girl's head, so she could hear her thoughts and feelings. Ryan had chosen the chair on purpose, not because it was assigned. It gave her a good vantage point of the whole classroom and still allowed her to see the board without her glasses. Her stepfather had knocked them off her face when he'd gotten home Saturday night. She needed them for her classes and she didn't know when her mom would be able to replace them. It all depended on her stepfather and when he would decide that she could see again. She pulled her notebook from her backpack and the small paperback of Shakespeare's sonnets that she had picked up at the used bookstore for a dollar. That way she could write in it and make notes, which was forbidden in the textbooks. Her English teacher Mrs. Newman was at the blackboard writing questions about Sonnet 130. They'd studied Othello last semester, and she'd enjoyed the play but the sonnets really touched her. She couldn't imagine loving someone so much.

"All right settle down," Mrs. Newman said facing the class. "Who wants to read aloud for me?"

Ryan sank lower in her seat, not wanting to be chosen. She hated public speaking, hated the idea of her classmate's eyes on her. What if they noticed the bruises on her arms or at the base of her neck? The door to the classroom opened and Layla Blake walked in late. Mrs. Newman stopped speaking, put her hands on her hips and gave Layla a disapproving look that rolled off the girl like water off a duck's feathers.

"That's your second tardy this week, Layla," Mrs. Newman said.

"Noted," Layla said and took the empty seat behind Ryan. Mrs. Newman went easy on Layla. Anyone else would've gotten a tardy slip and been sent to detention. It was almost like she had some sort of spell over Mrs. Newman, or maybe it was because Layla loved Shakespeare, and could talk about things that no one else in the class could. Some people around school were afraid of Layla. Not because she was smart, but because she played with dangerous things — there were rumors that she was into Satanism and witchcraft. Any time Layla crossed the most popular group, which was led by Madison Holt - Queen of the God Squad and founder of the local abstinence campaign, the word witch got thrown around. But it never seemed to bother Layla. What would it be like to be so cool that even bullies like Madison didn't get to you? Ryan would never know. She did whatever it took to stay out of Madison's way.

Madison Holt sat two rows over and stared at Layla.

Ryan tried to ignore her, instead focusing on Mrs. Newman's voice and the imagery of Sonnet 130.

"You know I've got something that'll take care of that," Layla whispered.

Ryan cast a glance over her shoulder. "Are you talking to me?"

"Yeah." Layla grazed her finger over the back of Ryan's neck beneath her ponytail. Ryan shuddered at the touch and pulled away.

"Stop that," Ryan said. "I'm trying to pay attention."

"He got you good, huh?" Layla said.

A cold rock dropped into Ryan's stomach and she met Layla's gaze. "I don't know what you're talking about. I can't afford a bad grade in this class." Ryan pulled the collar of her white T-shirt up. Trying to cover the fading bruises at the back of her neck.

"I get it," Layla said, leaning forward, lowering her voice. "I had a step dad once, too."

"Who said anything about my step dad?" Ryan hissed.

"You know people talk. They talk a lot actually."

Ryan swallowed hard and stared into Layla's face. There was no pity, thank God. Just a sense of understanding.

"Ryan," Mrs. Newman said. "Would you like to share whatever you're talking about with the class?"

Ryan jerked toward Mrs. Newman, horrified that she'd been called out. Ryan sat up straight and cleared her throat. "No ma'am."

"Okay then, no talking in class."

"Yes, ma'am," Ryan said, turning toward the front of the class. From the corner of her eyes Ryan saw Madison Holt wearing a condescending look on her heart-shaped face. Madison pursed her perfectly plump lips and held her cell phone just underneath the desk as she texted something to the girl in front of her, Olivia Martin. They both cast a glance her way. Ryan forced herself to look at the board, at Mrs. Newman, anywhere except at Madison and Olivia. She didn't need to be noticed. Especially not for making "friends" with weirdo Layla Blake, with her dyed jet-black hair, her black clothes, and shiny black fingernails. Layla who had pentacles drawn on the back of her notebook.

No, she didn't need that kind of heat. So she kept her eyes on her own paper and listen to Mrs. Newman drone on and on about the dark lady in Shakespeare's sonnet.

CHARLIE AWOKE WITH A START. SHE SAT UP, FLIPPED ON the light and dug through the drawer of her bedside table for a pad and pen. She quickly scribbled down the details of her dream that she could remember. Ryan's name — Whisnant. And the other girl with the black fingernails — Layla Blake. They were both at Palmetto Point High School. Was that for real or just a construct of her mind? There was only one way to find out. She would have to go back to high school. That thought sent a fresh wave of cold dread through her stomach. She had hated high school.

A cross between a purring and gurgling sound made her look toward the corner where the ghost of Penny the chicken was roosting. The hen had her eyes closed and kept opening and closing her beak as if she was drawing in deep breaths, causing the faux snoring sound. Spirits often kept their habits from life. She guessed it was no different for the chicken. Even though it really didn't need to sleep. Or snore. Charlie got up out of bed and went into the kitchen to get a glass of water. She turned the light on over the sink and took a clean glass out of the drainer and filled it. The cool water washed the arid feeling out of her mouth she often got after a strange dream. Her heart leapt into her throat and she peered out the window. She could see an apparition of a man in the woods.

She quickly turned off her light. Maybe her eyes were playing a trick on her. After her eyes adjusted, though, she could see him glowing plain as day along the edge of the woods. He had gotten through the first line of defense of wards around the property and was now pressing up against the second. If he somehow managed to break through, there would be no stopping him. He would be able to get to her. Charlie checked the clock on the wall above the small bistro table. Its glow-in-the-dark hands read 2 AM. Charlie scrambled to find her phone she'd left charging in the living room.

She quickly rattled off a text to her cousin Jen, unsure if Jen had her phone with her. She knew she wouldn't be awake. She was probably sleeping deeply and who could blame her? Jen would be up in a couple of hours to go into work. Charlie watched the 6-inch screen of her phone, waiting for any sign that Jen was responding. But none came. She was on her own.

"Think, Charlie," she whispered to herself. Then she remembered the Gods-eye cross she'd made for dealing with a vengeful spirit last year. It was a simple cross made of sticks from the yard and yarn. Jen had shown her how to wrap the yarn in between the cross-like structure of the sticks. It was essentially a trap meant to capture the spirit until it could be released some place safe, like holy ground, or in her case, she'd given it to Tom and he had taken the spirit onward to wherever it was supposed to go.

She went into her living room. On one wall underneath the bank of windows was her sofa and a big cushy chair. And across from the sofa on the other side of the room was a large duck egg blue dresser. It had taken her two whole days to paint the dresser

WENDY WANG

with chalk paint and then another two days to wax and buff it. It was her favorite piece of furniture, other than her old spindle bed, which she had inherited from her grandmother Bunny. She used it as a television stand and a place to store extra towels and blankets. But the top center drawer was a catchall that held mostly stuff that didn't have a home, like stamps, and plumbers tape, a flashlight, a set of screwdrivers, and lots of little junk. She pilfered through it trying to remember where she had put the Gods-eye cross. It wasn't there. She scanned the room quickly. Where had she put it? She spotted the old trunk that she used as a coffee table. She went over to it and lifted the old brass latch, pulling the lid open. Sitting on top of a stack of spell books that had belonged to her grandmother Bunny was an extra God's-eye cross. Charlie grabbed it and held it to her chest.

Charlie tried to remember the simple spell that went with it. It had been several months since she'd needed to use one. And she had no doubt that the spirit wouldn't go down without a huge fight. One cross might not be enough. She looked down at her phone hoping to see a message from her cousin but there was nothing.

She took a deep breath. Tom had told her that if she needed him, he would be there. All she had to do was call his name and if he were in his reaper form, he would come. Well, she wasn't crazy about seeing him in that form. Nothing was quite as terrifying as staring into the face, if you could call it that, of a reaper.

Nevertheless, she said his name aloud. "Tom?" Her voice shook a little. "Tom, are you there?"

Charlie listened to every little sound waiting for any sign that he had heard her. Something scraped on the window over the couch, drawing her gaze. The spirit, through sheer force of will, had somehow pushed through the boundaries that her cousin had set up around the property. The spirit stared at her with a gleeful leer on his face. He was enjoying frightening her. Is this what he had done to his step-daughter? Terrified her? No wonder she wanted to curse him. He pushed his hand through the window and then his whole body followed suit.

"Hello, witch," he said. "Are you ready to pay?"

Charlie held out the God's-eye cross and began the incantation. "Goddess of the moon and sun, I call upon your aid. Put the spirit where he belongs, with others like him, let him fade.

Earth, wind, fire and air, return this spirit whence he came and soothe his anger and his fear. So, mote it be."

The antique iron floor lamp that she had gotten in an estate sale and restored herself, lifted into the air and flew at her, interrupting her incantation. She dove out of the way just in time to see it smash into her television and leave a wide gash in the top edge of her dresser. Charlie gritted her teeth and held up the cross again. "You bastard. That's my favorite piece of furniture."

The trunk slid across the floor toward her and she rolled out of the way, but not quite fast enough. It clipped her elbow and her hand opened as an electric spark of nerves traveled from her elbow down to her fingers. She cried out and dropped the God's-eye cross.

"When are you going to learn? You're just like her. You think you're better than me. Well I'm dead, witch, and I can see the world. You think your stupid little protections will stop me? Nothing can stop me. You can ask Ryan if you don't believe me. Your little charm necklace was worthless," he said, hovering over her.

He held his hand out just over her neck and began to squeeze. A fresh wave of pain went through her throat and she tried to scream but the only thing that would come out of her mouth was a gurgling sound. Charlie clawed at the invisible hand around her neck but it was useless.

A strange screeching clucking sound and a flapping of wings filled the air. He loosened his grip on her throat and turned toward the sound just as Penny the hen flew at him, feet and spurs first. She flew right through him and he backed off.

"What the fuck?" he said, swiping at the air.

Charlie flipped over on all fours, coughing and crawling for the God's-eye cross. The hen disappeared. Charlie grabbed the cross and held it up and began her incantation again. The spirit-man scowled and turned on her. He raised his hand, and the television levitated. He pulled his arm back almost as if he were going to throw a ball at her. Charlie continued her incantation, and he began to flicker. The television dropped and crashed onto the dresser. He started to scream and curse at her. She got to her feet and held the cross out, more determined than ever to stop him forever. Behind her she heard her front door burst open. Charlie dropped her arm, halfway expecting to find Tom. But a man she had never seen before stepped inside.

"Get behind me," he said, and he pulled a glowing gold amulet from his pocket.

The spirit dove for the window, disappearing into the night.

"What the actual hell?" Charlie yelled. "You let him escape! I had him. And look what you did to my door!"

"Sorry about that. Don't worry I'll fix it. It will look brand-new by the time I'm finished with it," he said, turning to face her. He was tall, at least six feet two by her estimation. And he had a round, boyish face but there were determined lines carved into his forehead and he wielded that amulet like only a witch could.

"Who the hell are you?"

He smiled an easy smile, and she knew immediately that it was part of his persona. A weapon to charm and disarm. Scott, her ex-husband, had that same sort of smile that he used to pull out whenever he wanted something from her.

He held out his hand. "You called the Defenders of Light. I was the closest agent in the area. I'm Ben Sutton."

Charlie crossed her arms over her breasts, suddenly aware that she was only wearing a cotton nightgown. She shifted her feet.

"Do you always make your house calls at 3 AM?"

"You weren't supposed to know I was here. If it weren't for the spirit, you never would have."

"Oh, I don't know about that," she said. "So are you a medium? Is that why you could see him?"

"Nope, I'm not. I'm not a conduit like you evidently are. I'm a necromancer. Spirits only come to me when I call them. I take it you're more at their mercy."

"I'm not at anybody's mercy, dead or alive," Charlie said defensively.

"Whatever you say, honey," he smirked.

She wasn't sure if it was his tone or the simper on his lips but something about him rubbed her the wrong way. "I'm not your honey."

He chuckled. "Sorry about that. I thought that was the norm down here."

"Only if you're *from* here, which obviously you're not."

"No, I certainly am not." He let his eyes wander around the room. "You have quite a mess here. Would you like me to help you pick it up?"

"No thank you."

"You sure? I can have this place restored in a jiffy."

"How?"

He furrowed his brow. "You're a witch, right?"

"Yes," she said, tightening her arms across her chest. "That doesn't mean that the world bows down to me, though."

"Then you're doing it wrong, honey," he said, giving her the half smile that irritated her.

"I do not need you lecturing me on how to perform my craft. I can't believe that you are the representative of the Defenders of Light. I thought—" she stopped.

"You thought what?"

"Nothing," Charlie said, shaking her head. "I think you should go."

"I'm not going anywhere, sweetheart. I've been

chasing this witch across the country. I finally tracked her when I get word there's a witch in the area who's had a vision about my perp."

"Your perp," she scoffed. She'd never heard Jason use that term when talking about different perpetrators. He always said suspect.

"Yeah, my perp. Do you have a problem with that?" He stepped closer, and she looked him in the eye.

A hissing sound came from behind them and Charlie turned just in time to see the reaper's robes move past her as he swooped into the room, grabbed Ben by the throat, and pushed him up against a wall.

"Tom!" Charlie rushed forward, panic squeezing her heart. "No! He's a witch!"

Tom looked over his shoulder at her and hissed. It took everything she had not to cower at that sound and at that moment she realized with Tom in his natural form she had no idea how he would behave if threatened.

"Tom, please. Just let him go. He's here because I asked him."

Tom's long, thin skeletal-like fingers released the man, letting him drop to the floor.

"Holy shit," Ben said, rubbing his shoulder where Tom had picked him up like a rag doll. "You called a reaper on me?"

"No, of course not. I didn't call him on you. I

called him to help me with that spirit." Charlie turned to Tom. "Could you please go into my bedroom and change. It would make it much easier for everyone I think."

"Of course," Tom said, his silky voice sliding across her senses.

"It's right through there." Charlie pointed to the door of her bedroom and Tom glided across the floor, his robes fluttering behind him as if a fresh, cool breeze followed him around.

Charlie caught Ben staring at her in awe. "What?"

Ben shook his head. "Nothing."

A moment later Tom appeared fully clothed wearing his glamour.

"Holy shit," Ben muttered under his breath.

"Tom, this is Ben Sutton. He's a witch. He works for the Defenders of Light," Charlie said. "He's here because I asked them to help us find this witch that cast the curse."

"I see." Tom regarded Ben with caution. "I apologize for not getting here sooner. I heard your call, but I was tied up with something. Are you all right?"

"I'm fine. Thank you. I actually had it under control until he showed up. I was about to capture the spirit with a God's-eye cross, but he let him get away."

"It was a slight miscalculation on my part," Ben

said. "I thought she was in mortal danger. That's why I intervened."

"I'm sure. Did you do this?" Tom asked, pointing to all the damage in her living room."

"No," Ben said. "I'm only responsible for the door. The rest was all that nasty spirit."

"How did it get onto the property? I thought Evangeline had locked it up tight," Tom asked.

"I don't know," Charlie said.

"Hey, if the spirit wants to get in some place and it still has enough emotion fueling it, there's no ward in the world that will hold it back. Even salt can only protect to a certain extent," Ben chimed in. "The only thing I've ever seen that could keep the spirit contained is this."

Ben pulled his gold amulet from his pocket. Charlie could feel it across the room pulsing with energy. She had never seen anything like it before.

"Where did you get that?" Charlie asked.

"Egypt." Ben held it up and they could see it glowed faintly. He palmed it and put it back into his pocket. "On my very first mission for the DOL."

"Oh," Charlie said.

"So you're a witch?" Tom asked.

"I am. A highly trained, exceptionally skilled witch," Ben said.

"Well it's good to see that you don't lack self-confidence," Charlie said wryly.

"Well least I understand my powers. Which is more than I can say for you."

"What's that supposed to mean?" She shifted her stance, putting her hands on her hips to challenge him.

"Exactly what you think it means," Ben said.

"I think you should leave now," Charlie said. "But you need to fix my door first."

"Fine," Ben said. "I'll contact you in the morning. Then I'll take your statement and you don't have to worry about this case any longer."

"We'll that's not happening. I plan on seeing this through to the end."

"That's not how I work, honey," Ben said. "And you would do well not to interfere with a DOL investigation."

"Now wait a minute ..." Charlie started.

"No, Charlie, he's right." Tom took Charlie by the elbow and pulled her back a step. "You should give him your statement and then let him do his work."

Charlie glared at Tom, giving him a have-you-lost-your-mind look.

There is another way. Tom's silky reaper voice slid through Charlie's brain. She shook her head, a little unsure if she had heard him say that out loud or just in her mind. The voice spoke again. *There is another way. Trust me.* She was staring at Tom's lips and they had not moved so it had to be in her head.

"Fine. Have it your way." She turned to Ben. "I'll meet you at the Kitchen Witch Café tomorrow at 9 AM. Don't be late because I have to be at work by 11."

Ben shook his head. "I was thinking we would do this in a more private place."

"No way," Charlie said. "This has to be someplace public. I don't trust you. For all I know you could mess with my memory and I'm not having that."

Ben's jaw tightened, and he blew out an audible sigh. "Fine. The Kitchen Witch Café it is."

Charlie watched as he turned to her front door. He held his hands out and a glowing green plasma began to circle each of his fists. He stretched his fingers forward directing them toward the door. The splinters came flying off the floor, rejoining the wood until they were one piece again. The cracks in the white paint married together forming a perfectly smooth surface, and it looked as if the injury to the door had never occurred. When he was done, he closed his fingers and the green light dissipated like mist on a sunny day.

"See? All better." He smiled wide, his charm apparent again. Charlie bristled. "I'll see you at 9 AM on the dot."

He turned and walked out the door closing it tight behind him.

Charlie blew out a breath. "Well that was just the most bizarre experience I think I've ever had."

"That's saying a lot," Tom said, grinning. "I truly am sorry that I didn't get here in time to capture the spirit."

"It's okay," Charlie said. "I'm sorry I didn't catch him. It would've made it easy for you to transport him."

"Indeed," Tom said. "So you'll be working tomorrow I take it?"

"I will. I have to work from 11 to 7 tomorrow. Why?"

"I wanted to show you something related to your curse." Tom walked to the door, inspecting Ben's handiwork.

"Why didn't you tell Ben when he was here?"

He turned back to Charlie, apparently satisfied the door would hold. "For the same reason you didn't want to meet him in private. I don't trust him."

"All right. What is it you want to show me?"

"I received Debra Duguid's body tonight. That's why I didn't hear you immediately. I was working on her."

A chill raced down Charlie's spine. The image of Tom slicing into Debra's body and draining it of its blood flashed through her head. She shuddered.

"Okay," Charlie said. "I'm not quite following you. What does that have to do with the curse?"

"Her official cause of death was a stroke. But I have reason to believe that she was actually murdered. Just not in the typical fashion."

"What makes you say that?" she asked, alarm tingling along her arms.

"Because she has a glowing mark on her head. I've only seen something like it one other time about 100 years ago. I was working in England at the time. In a small village and a man who had died was brought to me. He had a very similar mark on his chest. Everyone in the village was convinced he had been cursed by a local woman they believed to be a witch."

"What happened to her? The woman they thought was a witch?"

"Not long after that she disappeared. No one knows where to or why. But everyone was relieved that she was gone."

Charlie shuddered again and took a deep breath.

"You must be exhausted."

"I am. It's almost 4 o'clock, though. I'm tempted to just stay up. I used to do that when Evan was a baby. He'd wake me up at 3 o'clock for a feeding and I wouldn't bother going back to bed. I would finally sleep when he slept." Charlie settled her gaze on Tom who was watching her thoughtfully. "What?"

"Nothing. I just ... I really like it when you tell me

stories like that. It makes me feel like we're really friends."

"We are really friends, Tom. And I like it when you share stories with me, too, even if they are a little creepy sometimes." She chuckled and wiped her eyes with her palms.

"I should probably go and let you get some sleep."

Panic wrapped around her heart and gave it a squeeze. She reached for his hand. "No. Wait."

Tom looked down in wonder at her hand holding his.

"What if he comes back?" she said.

"The spirit?" Tom said.

Charlie nodded.

"Would you like me to stay? I could ..." He glanced around toward the couch. "I could straighten things up while you sleep. I don't have any magic but I can certainly clean."

"No, you don't have to do that. I'll clean it up in the morning. I think I would just feel better knowing you were here." Charlie gave him a sheepish smile. "That is if you don't mind staying."

"I'd be happy to." He surprised her by giving her hand a squeeze.

"I feel like I'm six years old but I'm gonna ask you anyway. Do you think you could lie with me until I fall asleep?"

Tom's eyes widened and his lips curved into a slight smile. "I would be happy to. No funny business, I promise."

"Can reapers even ... you know ..." Charlie stumbled, unsure exactly how to ask her question.

"In this form? Oh yeah," Tom said softly.

"So you've ..." Charlie's cheeks heated. "You know."

"I have," he said, his smile growing brighter. "This has turned into a very interesting conversation."

"What? You said I could ask you questions. It's not an invitation. More of a request for information," she said, unable to suppress a laugh.

"All right then. Did that answer your question?"

"Yes."

"Good. Come on then," he said pointing back toward the bedroom. "Let's get you into bed."

CHAPTER 10

Charlie awoke to the smell of fresh coffee and eggs cooking. Light streamed in through the window of her small bedroom and she raised her arms above her head and stretched her back. She glanced at the clock on her bedside table and remembered the feel of Tom's arms around her as she fell asleep. A smile stretched her lips. She could not remember the last time she'd been in the arms of a man.

But he's not a man, a small voice said. *He's a reaper.*

Her smile faded from her lips and she pushed the quilt down and got out of bed before the voice could do anymore damage to her mood. She dressed quickly in a pair of jeans and a crisp, white T-shirt. She swept her long hair into a messy bun on the back of her head and ambled into the kitchen.

"Good morning," she said.

"Good morning," Tom said scraping scrambled eggs from the cast-iron pan onto a plate. "I've seen you eat this at the café on rare occasions. I didn't know how to make banana pancakes."

Charlie laughed. "That's okay. I don't know how to make them either. Those are Jen's specialty. I only eat things like pancakes and muffins at the café. I'm not exactly what you would call a cook."

"Good," he said. "I was afraid it might be too understated."

"No," she smiled. "Scrambled eggs are perfect. And so is fresh coffee." She pulled two mugs from the shelf and poured herself a cup. "I have tea bags in the cupboard if you'd like tea."

"Coffee's fine," he said. She nodded and filled his mug with coffee then put them both on the small bistro table. Tom placed the plate of scrambled eggs next to her mug. Charlie dug a fork out of the drawer next to the stove, then took a seat and gobbled down the eggs before they had a chance to get cold.

"These are really good," she said. "I always have to be careful with eggs because I burn them really easily and my son won't eat them at all if they have even the slightest bit of brown on them."

"Good to know. And I'm glad that you like them." He smiled watching her eat.

"Are you going to eat something?"

"Technically I don't really need to eat, just like I don't need to sleep," he said. "Although I do enjoy food quite a bit."

"All this time that you've been coming into the café for meals ..." she said.

"It's mainly because I enjoy human company. And Jen is particularly nice to me. And since you have forgiven me you're pretty nice too."

Charlie tried to suppress a smile but found it almost impossible to keep her lips from curving up. She tipped her head forward and finished off her eggs.

"That was delicious. I guess we should get going. You still wanted show me the mark, right?"

"Yes," he said. "Especially if it will help you."

* * *

CHARLIE DROVE THEM INTO TOWN AND PARKED around back of the mortuary next to Tom's black Ford Fusion. She followed him into the building down a hallway she had never seen before until they came to a pair of double doors. Tom put his hand out as if to push the door open and Charlie panicked.

"Wait," her voice squeaked.

Tom stopped and shifted his attention to her. He gave her a quizzical look. "What's wrong?"

"I don't think I can go in there," Charlie said pressing her hands to her belly.

"Are you feeling ill?" he asked.

"No it's not that. It's just ... you want me to look at Debra Duguid's dead body. And that is ... terrifying. I mean Debra was not a pleasant person in life. What if her spirit's in there? I don't know if I'm up for dealing with Debra's contrariness this morning. Especially if it's magnified, which you know happens after someone dies."

"Very true," Tom said. "I hadn't thought about that. Although, here's something to think about. If she is in there, I will transform quickly. It usually only takes a few seconds. Then I can capture her before she can rage against you."

Charlie nodded. "All right, if you're sure you can do it that quickly."

"I can. I promise I won't let her hurt you."

"Just make sure you transform before she can hurt you. Seeing your human form be injured in any way is ..." she sighed. "Well it's disturbing. More disturbing than just seeing you transform I think."

"Noted," he said. "And thank you for telling me that. I feel like we're really making progress in this ... friendship of ours."

Charlie gave him a sly smile. "Yes, I guess you could say that. Okay, let's go ahead and do this."

Tom gave her a quick nod and pushed the door

open. He walked in ahead of her and scanned the room. "The coast is clear as they say. There doesn't appear to be any sign of her."

"Thank god for that," Charlie said walking into the room. Her breath caught in her throat at the site of the old woman lying face up on the metal table and she stopped in her tracks. Her hand drifted to her mouth, keeping the scream from passing her lips. She crept forward slowly.

"She can't hurt you," Tom said. "You've seen dead bodies before, haven't you?"

"Yes. Of course, I have. They just usually are in a casket and have some color in their face. I didn't realize how ..." Charlie swallowed hard. "Bloodless she would look. I mean I saw that man who attacked me. But even he had more color." Charlie sidled up next to the table staring down at Debra. Her silver hair looked whiter than she remembered. "Why does she look so puffy?"

"The tissues swell sometimes with the embalming fluid and she'll have more color tomorrow. We have a makeup artist who will put a little life back into her skin and dress her."

"I think this is the most peaceful I've ever seen her look. I don't see the mark. I thought you said it was on her head," Charlie said.

"Right," Tom said. "The whole reason we are here. Help me get her onto her side."

"What?" Charlie took a step back and her lips twisted with disgust.

"Don't worry. I'll do most of the touching. All I need for you to do is lift her hair at the very back of her neck once I get her onto her side. Are you okay with that?"

Charlie grimaced and nodded. "Okay. I can do that."

Tom carefully shifted Debra's body onto her left side. Charlie combed Debra's soft, white hair to the side. She could see the faint glow of the death mark at the base of her skull.

"Yep," Charlie said grimly. "That's it. Dammit. I want to find who's doing this, but I sure don't want to have to work with that jerk, Ben."

"Assuming he's even more open to it. Which it doesn't sound like he is. I suppose there's no way to get your deputy friend to help."

"Nope. Debra died from a stroke. And the spirit who has it in for me, well he died from a head injury. Neither of which are a crime. I guess Jason's department's cutting down on unnecessary expenditures."

"You may not have a choice then." Tom said.

"We'll see what I can negotiate. I think there are still things I do that he can't, no matter how skilled he thinks he is."

"You go girl," Tom said

Charlie laughed and shook her head. "I'm going

to say the same thing that my son says to me when I think I'm being cool. Don't ever say that again."

Tom feigned being hurt as he gently laid Debra back down on the table. He fussed with the sheet covering the deceased woman's body until it was smooth.

"You know what?" Charlie said.

"What? Tom said.

"I think you really like human beings."

"Why do you say that?"

"Just the way you are so gentle and respectful of the dead." She met his gaze without flinching. "And of the living. I think that's why you put that face on. It's not really to help you catch spirits. You're much more effective in your reaper form at capturing the dead."

Tom pressed his lips together and nodded his head thoughtfully. "Maybe you're right. Maybe that's exactly why I like being in human form. Because despite all your shortcomings there is still something incredibly admirable about your drive and spirit. I can never be human but when I wear this skin, I feel almost like I could be human by association."

Charlie's phone chirped signaling she had a text. She ignored it until her phone began to vibrate. "I'm sorry." She glanced down at the phone, worried it might be her son. The name Jason Tate flashed across her screen. She frowned. "I need to take this, I'm sorry. It's Jason." She pressed the green button and answered hello.

"I'm sorry to bother you this early. But I thought you would want to know. Two bodies were discovered last night with broken necks."

Charlie's heart turned into a cold rock and dropped into her belly. "Oh my God. Please don't tell me."

"Yes, it was the girl Ryan Whisnant and her mother. There doesn't appear to be a break-in. In fact the doors were locked."

The dream came back to Charlie, Ryan trying to hide her bruises. "But you think they were murdered?"

"It's looking that way. I can't call it until the corner does, but broken necks don't just happen by themselves," Jason said.

"Well you should know that he showed up at my house last night."

"The ..." Jason fell silent but Charlie filled in the word that he couldn't say.

"Ghost."

"Are you all right?"

"Yes. I'm fine. But we also have another curse victim."

"Who?"

"Debra Duguid. The wife of Palmetto Point's illustrious mayor."

"Charlie! I thought she died from a stroke."

"She did. But she also has the mark at the base of her skull. I would bet you that if we opened her skull up that mark would coincide with the bleed in her brain."

"Well you wanted to me to be involved. I now have something to investigate."

Charlie rubbed her forehead and squeezed her eyes shut. "I know but not this way. I didn't want anybody to have to die."

"I know," he said. "I was hoping you could run through the scene with me after the forensic guys are done."

"Sure. It will have to be tonight or tomorrow though. I've got to go to work at eleven."

"Okay. I'll text you later and we'll figure out a time."

"Thanks for letting me know."

"Sure thing," Jason said and ended the call. Charlie stared at her phone until she felt Tom's warm hand touch her in the middle of the back.

"What happened?"

"Ryan Whisnant, the girl I told you about. She and her mother are dead. I guess I know what he meant now."

"Who?"

"Tony Smoak. The dead man who attacked me. He said something about his step-daughter last night, but everything happened so fast. I should have known then what he meant."

"How could you?" Tom said, "You're too hard on yourself."

"You still think humans are admirable?" Charlie sighed.

He smiled. "Some humans. Yes."

She tucked her phone into her back pocket and considered Tom's face. He was still handsome enough to make her heart ache when she looked at him. Would that ever wear off? Some part of her hoped it never would. "I need to go to meet with the DOL guy."

"All right. Talk soon?"

Charlie nodded and backed away, smiling. "Talk soon."

CHAPTER 11

Charlie left her car at the mortuary and walked the three blocks down the street to The Kitchen Witch Café. Even this early there were still plenty of people on the street but Charlie couldn't shake the feeling of being watched. She kept scanning her surroundings and glancing over her shoulder. What would happen if Tony Smoak attacked her on the street? No one would be able to help her. She quickened her pace. As much as she hated to admit it, she felt safer knowing there was at least one witch in the vicinity that could stop him.

She saw Ben Sutton through the window sitting at the counter, leaning forward. He had his eyes on her cousin Jen and something yawned inside of her. Something fierce and protective. She walked through the front door, the bell jingling behind her. Even though things wouldn't get really going until Memorial Day, the café was bustling at this time of the morning with tourists and locals alike. Charlie marched up to Ben.

"What are you doing?" she said, her voice sharp and filled with accusation.

"Well good morning to you, too." Ben turned his head and gave her an appraising look.

"Charlie! Don't be rude," Jen said, sounding mortified. She glanced back and forth at the two of them. They glared at each other and her face filled with confusion. "Do you two know each other?"

"Know is a little strong," Charlie said.

"We became acquainted last night. How do you two know each other?" Ben asked.

"This is my cousin," Charlie said, aware that she sounded almost territorial.

"Of course she is," Ben said dryly.

"Charlie?" Jen's tone was a little curt. "May I speak with you please? Now."

"Of course." Charlie glared at Ben. "I'll be right back."

"And I'll be right here." He reached for his coffee.

Charlie walked around to the end of the counter and followed her cousin into the kitchen.

"Charlie, how exactly do you know Ben?"

"He didn't tell you?" Charlie lowered her brows,

suspicion in her question.

"No. What should he have told me?"

Charlie glanced around to see who was in the kitchen. Evangeline was too busy at the grill to notice and the other two waitresses that worked for Jen kept buzzing in and out of the kitchen, paying them no mind.

Still, Charlie leaned in and whispered, "He's a witch."

"No." Jen said shaking her head. "I would have known if he was a witch. He's nice."

It was on the tip of her tongue to say *bless your heart* but Charlie knew it was a good way to start a fight and she had already alienated Lisa. She didn't want to do the same thing with Jen.

"Honey, he's a witch. I went to Evangeline the other day and we contacted the Defender's of Light. Long story short, I was in the middle of an attack last night."

"What do you mean? An attack?"

"Well ..." Charlie took a deep breath. "I'm afraid that Tony Smoak, the spirit who attacked me in my car? Somehow he broke through the boundaries last night. Ben seems to think it was the spirit's will."

"What?"

"Did you not see my text?" Charlie asked.

"I ..." Jen shook her head no. "I'm sorry I didn't even look at my phone this morning before I left."

Her hand flew to her mouth in concern. "What happened?"

Charlie ran through the events of last night ending with Ben showing up and blowing her chance at capturing Tony Smoak. She didn't mention Tom though. She would leave that subject for another time.

"That Ben out there?" Jen pointed to the door.

"I'm sorry, honey. But yeah," Charlie said.

Jen's face filled with disappointment.

Charlie wrapped her arms around Jen and gave her a gentle squeeze, her voice incredulous as she spoke, "You like him."

"He flirted with me. Even asked me on a date." Jen stepped back, staring into Charlie's face. "No point in going if he works for the DOL."

"Why not?" Charlie said softly.

"They're nomads. Never in one place for very long."

"I'm sorry honey," Charlie said.

"It just felt good. That's all." Jen's lips pulled into a frown. "It's been a long time since I've been on a date."

"I know."

"It doesn't matter. Come on. Let's go talk to him." Jen turned to the busy kitchen. "Evangeline, I think we're gonna need you."

Evangeline gave them a puzzled look then said

something neither of them could hear to the new sous chef she was training. The three women emerged from the kitchen and Ben straightened up, the lines in his forehead growing deep as they approached him.

"Well this looks serious," Ben said. "I'm not sure what she told you Jen—"

"She told me the truth," Jen said. "Which I'm afraid is more than you did, Ben."

Ben frowned. "Now wait a minute." He glanced around at the busy restaurant. "I was not in a position to be totally upfront with you."

"I think that's secondary to the matter," Evangeline said. "I take it that you are the help we requested?"

Ben stood up. "Yes," he said. "I thought you were just one of the cooks."

"I am one of the cooks. I'm also one of the owners and these two women are my nieces," Evangeline said.

Ben nodded his head. "A family business. Does everything run in the family?"

"Yes," Charlie said. "It does. But I believe you knew that already. So let's just get to the point, shall we?"

Evangeline glanced around at the crowd. "Why don't we head to the back office? It's less likely we'll be overheard there."

"Now that's the best idea I've heard all morning," Ben said.

"Come with me," Evangeline said. Ben, Charlie and Jen followed Evangeline through the kitchen doors past the kitchen, past the walk-in freezer and storeroom to the tiny back office where Jen did their books and ordered inventory. Evangeline opened the door and gestured for Ben to walk in first. A small desk with the computer took up most of the back wall. A small television was perched on top of the printer stand and there were only two chairs. An office chair and a ladder-backed wooden chair pushed into one of the corners.

"Please have a seat," Evangeline said.

Ben walked in and looked around. "Nice set-up you have here." He took a seat in the office chair. Charlie pulled the ladder-backed chair away from the wall and offered it to Evangeline.

"No, thank you," Evangeline said serenely. "I'll stand."

Jen took the seat and folded her arms across her chest. She glared at Ben; the betrayal she felt filled every line of her face. Charlie took a seat on the edge of the desk and Evangeline closed the door and positioned herself behind Jen's chair, holding onto the top rung.

"I didn't expect this to be a family affair," Ben said.

"I didn't expect you to be so young," Evangeline said. "I thought for sure the DOL would send an experienced agent."

"Oh, you don't have to worry about that ma'am." Ben bristled and narrowed his eyes. "I'm very experienced. I just need to get some information from Charlie here about her complaint, what she's witnessed and this spirit who attacked her. Then I'll be out of your hair."

"I think you need more than my statement, Mr. Sutton," Charlie said. "I have some experience myself investigating these sorts of things. I think you could use my help."

"Well I appreciate that, honey but ..."

"I thought we had settled this. Do not call me honey," Charlie said firmly.

"Sorry. I appreciate that you think you have some experience. But from what I've seen, you lack training and discipline. And I work alone."

"Then why should I share anything with you?" Charlie said.

"You're the one that called me, sweetheart," he said.

"Mr. Sutton, I'm not gonna tell you again about using terms of endearment that you haven't earned," Charlie said. "Do it again, and you might just find your tongue tied in a knot. Literally."

"Fine," he said unruffled by her threat. "You

called for me because you suspect a witch is cursing people in your town. And I came. Now tell me what you know so I can catch the witch who's responsible."

"Well I've changed my mind. I don't think I need your help after all," Charlie said. "I have a contact in local law enforcement and a case that he received last night actually coincides with mine so we'll be working together. I'm sorry I wasted your time."

"That's not how this works. You and I both know that your," Ben held up his hand and made air quotes, *"local law enforcement* are useless when it comes to supernatural matters. I've already been here for two weeks looking for this witch. I know your deaths look natural and accidental. There's not a damn thing that local law enforcement can do for you."

"Well I have two murders in the mix now," Charlie said. "So I have all the resources I need."

"What murders?" Ben asked.

"A teenager and her mother were murdered last night. Their necks snapped," Charlie said.

"What does that have to do with my witch?"

"They were the stepdaughter and wife of the spirit that you, what was your word? Miscalculated capturing. He evidently killed them last night before he attacked me."

"Why are the police wasting their time looking for a spirit?"

"Technically they don't know it's a spirit."

"But you do," Ben said.

"Yes I do. And since I'm what you called a conduit, I'm hoping that their spirits are still hanging around. That way I can get some information and then help them cross over to where they need to be."

Ben locked his gaze on Charlie and pursed his lips. "I could call them. I am a necromancer after all."

"You're a necromancer?" Jen sounded slightly appalled. "I thought necromancers could only call spirits of their ancestors or spirits that they've already made connections with. You can't compel a spirit that doesn't know you. In fact you can't compel a spirit at all, right? All you can do is beseech a spirit and ask them for their help."

"Jen is correct," Evangeline said.

"Looks like you're not the only one that's highly trained around here." Charlie didn't even bother to suppress her righteous grin.

"I don't know you, Mr. Sutton," Evangeline said, her voice as calm as a mountain lake. "But if you have been in this area for two weeks, then I'm sure you've already done your research on us. My family has been here since the early 1700s. And we have produced hundreds of witches with the collective knowledge that has been passed down for over 300 years. So even though Charlie has only recently embraced her heritage as a witch, don't underestimate her. She's a natural witch. And she has a tremendous amount of power that she hasn't even begun to tap yet."

Ben's cheeks turned ruddy and his jaw tightened. "Well it looks like you don't need me at all then. I guess I'll be going. Jen it was really nice to meet you. Despite what you may think of me, I really did enjoy talking to you."

Ben got up from his chair and hiked up his jeans.

"Wait," Charlie said. "I think you and I *could* work together. But you'd have to open your mind a little."

"And you'd have to do what I said," Ben said, challenging her.

"You're not the first law man to ever have to tell me that."

"And how did that work out?" Ben asked, the corners of his mouth tugging into a wry grin.

"We're still working on it," Charlie said.

"I'm probably gonna regret this," Ben said. "And I'm not going to pay you."

"I don't expect you to." Charlie offered her hand. Ben took a deep breath and shook her it.

"All right, what can you tell me about these murders?" he asked.

CHAPTER 12

After Charlie clocked out at 7 PM, she walked down to the lobby and waited just inside the doorway until Jason pulled up in his black Dodge Charger. She walked out of the building, waved and then hopped in the front seat.

"You sure you want to do this tonight?" he said, putting his car into gear.

"Yes, I'm sure. There's something I need to talk to you about first, though," Charlie said.

"Okay, shoot," Jason said, easing away from the curb.

Charlie went on to explain how she had contacted the Defenders of Light for help when Jason told her that he couldn't investigate because technically the deaths of Tony Smoak and Deborah Duguid were not crimes.

"So the Defenders of Light have an investigative unit?" Jason said.

"Yes. And one of the investigators is in Palmetto Point. He's here to capture the witch responsible for the curses," Charlie said.

"What happens to her?" Jason asked.

"There'll be a tribunal and evidence will be presented. She will be allowed to defend herself and if she's found guilty, then she shall be stripped of her powers." Charlie looked away at the passing scene out her window as she reflected on dark witches.

"How does that work?" Jason asked.

"You don't want to know. Rather painful. From what Evangeline told me," she said.

"Who knew? So there's this whole shadow world. Witches, ghosts ..."

"Yep." Charlie nodded her head. "And demons and vampires." She gave him a side-eyed glance. Jason shifted uncomfortably in his seat.

"Okay, you're just joking about the vampire thing, right?"

"Whatever you say," she said, a sly grin on her face.

"No, I'm serious now." Jason twisted in his seat to check traffic but Charlie could see he was trying to disguise his agitation. "Vampires are just a thing that Bram Stoker made up, right?"

"What if I say no?"

"You're right, I don't want to know." Jason shook his head and gripped the wheel tighter. "Are there any here? You know, in the greater Charleston area?"

"Probably," Charlie said, unable to stop grinning. This was too much fun. "I personally don't know any that live here but that doesn't mean they don't. It just means I've never crossed paths with one."

Jason sighed heavily and shook his head.

"How's that shadow world looking to you now?" she teased.

"Shut up," Jason said.

She asked him for the address and then texted it to Ben Sutton once she and Jason were close to the Whisnant house. She would rather wait for Ben than have him get there first. She didn't need him snooping around on his own.

Jason parked in the driveway of the two-story house. Fresh crime scene tape formed an X over the door and Charlie could see a paper seal had been put into place to keep people out. She and Jason waited on the porch for Ben to arrive. A few minutes after she texted him he drove up on a motorcycle. He pulled into the driveway and parked next to Jason, took off his mirrored-black helmet and perched it on the seat.

He raised his hand in a wave as he approached them. And Charlie waved back.

"Deputy Jason Tate this is agent Ben Sutton of the Defenders of Light."

Ben held his hand out and Jason shook it. The two men sized each other up.

"Are you carrying a weapon?" Jason asked.

"Of course," Ben said. "But not the kind you are. Mine is not quite as destructive as a gun."

Jason kept his face neutral and nodded. Charlie had seen him do this before; he had an excellent poker face.

"The place has already been dusted for finger-prints," Jason said, pulling a few pairs of gloves out of his front pocket. "But since we're going to be looking for evidence, I would prefer that we all wear gloves. Do you have a problem with that?"

Ben shook his head and took a pair of gloves. "Not at all. This is your show."

"All right," Jason said.

Charlie accepted gloves from Jason and slipped them on, watching Jason take a small penknife from his front pocket and slice through the paper sealing the front door. He carefully removed one end of each of the strips of crime scene tape letting them hang down like party streamers. He turned the knob, and they entered the residence.

A chill immediately settled around Charlie's shoulders.

"They must've left the air conditioning on," Jason said, rubbing his hands together. "It's like a meat locker in here."

"The air-conditioning is not on," Ben said. He dug through his pocket and pulled out the gold amulet he'd shown Charlie last night.

Jason looked to Charlie for confirmation and she nodded. "He's right. This isn't from air-conditioning." Her breath puffed out in little silver clouds as she spoke. "There are spirits here."

Jason reached into the neck of his polo shirt and pulled his pendant out. "Where's your necklace, Charlie?"

"I gave it to her," Charlie said.

"Who?"

"The girl who lives here."

"The dead girl?" Jason asked.

"Yep." Charlie reached into the large leather bag she wore across her body. She pulled a red and black God's eye cross from the purse and held it at her side. "It's okay I have this."

"I can't believe you're using that," Ben muttered.

"Why wouldn't I? It works," she said.

"It's not a permanent trap."

"That's fine. I don't need it to be," Charlie said. "I know a reaper that can actually transport the soul to where it needs to go with one."

"Right," Ben said. He didn't hide his irritation. "One day you'll have to tell me the story of how you made friends with the reaper. I didn't think they were that friendly. They're usually all business."

Charlie rolled her eyes. "Maybe we should split up."

"Now there's an idea I can get behind," Ben said.

"I'm only suggesting it so that we can cover more ground. It's really not going to help matters if you decide to go all rogue and start collecting souls in your permanent amulet there," she snapped.

"I won't go rogue. You don't go rogue, either. We need to talk to the spirits," Ben said.

"Well, there's something we at least agree on," Charlie said.

"Fine," Ben snapped. "I'll take the upstairs."

"Great," Charlie said.

She and Jason watched as Ben split off and headed up the carpeted steps to the second floor.

Jason moved closer to her and spoke quietly. "So what's your plan?"

"My plan is to find them first. I saw the girl when we first came in the house. In the kitchen. She looked terrified," she said.

"So he can't see them?"

"He says he can but," she shrugged a shoulder. "I'm not sure I believe him. You up for this?"

"Of course I am," he said. "What about you?"

"Yep," she nodded. "Come on, let's go talk to her."

Charlie and Jason walked through the foyer to the open door of the kitchen. The air chilled even more and Charlie fought the urge to shiver.

"Ryan?" Charlie called. "I know you're here. And I know you're scared. I just want to help you."

A voice came from behind them. "Haven't you done enough helping?"

Jason's eyes scanned the room. "Did you hear that?"

"I did," Charlie said. "But I'm surprised you did."

"Yeah, me too," Jason mumbled.

"Ryan? Is that you?" Charlie called. A large knife block sat on the kitchen island next to a thick, expensive-looking butcher block. Charlie saw the knife handles begin to rattle in their slots. She reached for Jason's arm and pulled him to the floor as the first knife flew over their heads and planted into the wall behind them. "Ryan, do you remember me? We met not too long ago. You hid in my car." A stack of plates crashed onto the floor near Charlie's feet.

"Ryan, I know this is scary. You don't know what's happened to you. I can help you. Let me help you," Charlie said.

Charlie could hear Jason's harsh breath but there

were no other sounds in the room. Charlie peeked around the corner of the kitchen island. There was no sign of the girl.

"She's gone," Charlie said. "Come on." She stood up. Jason stayed on the floor.

"I really don't want a knife in the back, Charlie." Jason said. "Maybe I should just stay here."

"I need you with me," she said.

"Why? I can't even see her."

"I know but I still need your eyes and your senses. Just because you can't see her doesn't mean you can't feel her," she said. "You're also a pretty good negotiator."

Jason rolled his eyes. "Now you're just kissing my ass."

"Is it working?" she asked.

He smirked. "Maybe." He rose to his feet.

They heard a loud crash upstairs and rushed up the steps with Charlie in the lead. She held tightly to the God's-eye cross in her hand. She really didn't want to have to catch the girl with it. But she would if it came to that. They rounded the corner into what looked like the master bedroom, just in time to see Ben fly across the room and crash into the mirror over a large, expensive-looking dresser. The silvered glass cracked, and he landed on the ground, stunned, his amulet on the floor just out of his reach.

Charlie tucked the cross in her pocket and held

her hands up in surrender. "Hey," Charlie said, facing the apparition of a petite woman who looked a lot like Ryan. Her body flickered with most of her bottom half not showing at all. And what did show was transparent. "Hey there. You're Ryan's mom, right?"

"Who are you and what are you doing in my house?" she screeched.

"My name is Charlie Payne." Charlie used the voice she reserved for soothing upset customers. "I know you're scared and I know you're confused. I'm here to help you. But I need you to answer a few questions for me if that's possible."

The woman drifted closer and Charlie, out of the corner of her eye, saw Jason back away.

"There were men in my house all day," the apparition said.

"I know," Charlie said.

"And no one would answer my questions. It's like they didn't even see me," the woman said.

"What's your name?" Charlie asked.

"My name is Caroline. Caroline Smoak," she said.

"Caroline, it's nice to meet you," Charlie said. "Do you know what happened to you?"

"I remember ... I remember Tony. And I kept thinking this has to be a dream because Tony's dead. But he came in to the bedroom and he was so angry."

"Do you remember what happened after that?" Charlie asked.

"He ..." she stopped and closed her eyes as if saying it out loud was too painful.

Charlie stepped forward. "I'm sorry to have to tell you this but he killed you. That's why those men were here today. They were looking for evidence."

"I think I knew that. I just ..." Caroline crossed her arms hugging them tightly to herself and Charlie wondered if it was something she had done often in life. "I just didn't want to admit it to myself I think."

"I know," Charlie said. "I really need to talk to your daughter. She's hiding somewhere in this house, though. Do you think you could get her to talk to me? It's really important. It will help me put Tony to rest, and you too."

"Will we ... will we go to heaven?" Caroline asked.

"I certainly hope so," Charlie said, dropping her voice to a soothing register.

"Ryan, honey," Caroline called. "You can come out now. I don't think they're going to hurt us."

A second later Ryan flickered into the room and came to a halt next to her mother. Her body was a little more opaque.

"I'm afraid your blessing didn't work," Ryan said.

"I'm sorry about that," Charlie said. "I need to

know something, Ryan. Remember when you asked me for a curse?"

"Ryan?" her mother said, her tone full of shock.

"I was just trying to stop him from hurting us," Ryan said. "I didn't want him dead. Really, I didn't. I just wanted him to stop. Actually I wanted him to leave but I figured that wouldn't happen." Ryan folded her arms across her chest in a show of defiance.

In the corner Ben moaned and pushed onto all fours, shaking his head. Blood streamed down one side of his face. He must have hit the mirror with his forehead for it to bleed so badly. Charlie frowned and brought her attention back to the two apparitions in front of her.

"Ryan, I need to know who performed the curse for you? Where did you get the witch's ladder?"

Ryan's gaze flitted from her mother to Charlie and back. Her mother wore an expression of disappointment.

"It's okay, Ryan. Please, I need you to tell me. There's another lady who's died because of a curse. I need to stop whoever is making these curses. I don't want anyone else to die, do you?"

"Are you serious? Someone else has died?" Ryan asked.

"I am." Charlie nodded her head.

"I mean I didn't think she would be doing it for

more people. She didn't tell me it would kill my stepfather." She chewed her bottom lip. "I just wanted to
protect me and my mom."

"Oh sweetie, I am so sorry." Caroline reached out
to touch her daughter and it surprised Charlie when
the spirit was able to make what looked like physical
contact with Ryan. She had never seen that before.

"I probably wouldn't have done it if I'd known he
was gonna die, especially since we ended up dead
anyway," Ryan mumbled.

"I understand," Charlie said. "I just need
a name."

Ryan rolled her eyes and sighed. "Layla Blake.
She goes to my school. She's kind of a Goth girl,
weird and into witchcraft. Doesn't care what
anybody thinks." She sounded wistful as she spoke
of the other girl.

"Why would you make friends with somebody
like that?" her mother scolded.

"I don't know, maybe because I was desperate.
You were never going to leave him, were you?"

"Oh, Ryan, it wasn't quite that simple," her
mother said.

"You're right. She was never gonna leave me. She
knew I'd kill her if she tried. Didn't you, Caroline?"

Tony Smoak stood in the doorway, his apparition
almost solid. His energy was growing.

Charlie and Jason faced the spirit. She pulled the

Gods-eye cross out of the back pocket of her jeans as fast as she could, held it up and began her incantation. Ben finally came out of his stupor, grabbed his amulet off the floor and moved to her side, reciting his own incantation.

Ryan and her mother disappeared as shards of mirror began to fly around the room. Jason picked up a tray that had been dumped on the floor. Bottles and palettes of makeup lay broken on the carpet next to it. As Charlie and Ben worked to capture Tony's spirit, Jason batted at the sharp pieces of silvered glass, trying to keep them from hitting them.

The bed dragged across the floor and Jason jumped out of the way. Charlie's voice grew louder as she spoke the words of the incantation. She reached for Ben's hand, grabbing hold of it. She thought he might throw her off but he held on tight. His energy strengthened her, and her energy flowed into him; for a moment it sizzled through them both, reinforcing their collective power.

The spirit shook in place, flickering with shadows and light. He became soft around the edges and with one final scream his spirit body split into two—half going toward her cross and the other half into Ben's amulet. The shards of mirror dropped to the floor and an eerie silence fell over the house.

"I got him," Charlie said.

"You mean I got him," Ben said.

"Why does this have to be a competition? We both got him, okay?" Charlie said giving him an incredulous look.

"Fine, we both got him." Ben rolled his eyes. "I've never really seen that happen before. I can't imagine a fractured spirit is going to be a good thing, though."

"It's fine. We can deliver him to Tom and he can take him to where he's supposed to go."

"That's your reaper friend, right?"

"Yep." Charlie turned to Jason. "Are you all right?"

"Is he gone?" Jason dropped the tray on the floor.

Charlie nodded. "Yeah, he's gone." Ryan and her mother reappeared. Jason jumped back, startled by the two spirits.

"What happens to us?" Caroline asked.

"I have a friend who's going to take you on," Charlie said. "I'm going to call him now. He may be a little scary at first, but I don't want you to be afraid. I promise he won't hurt you."

Ryan moved closer to her mother. Fear made their bodies flicker.

"Tom," Charlie said. "Tom can you hear me?" They waited for a moment and finally Tom materialized behind her.

"Charlie," Tom said in a silky voice. "Is everything all right?"

"Yes. We caught Tony Smoak." She handed Tom the God's-eye cross, and he slipped it inside his robe. "This is Ryan and her mother Caroline." Tom regarded the two quaking spirits in front of him. "I told them that you were going to take them onward, where they need to be. That you wouldn't hurt them."

Tom's robed head nodded. He held out his arm. "Grasp on to my robe," he instructed them.

Ryan threw one last glance at Charlie and took hold of Tom's robe along with her mother. A pang of sadness squeezed Charlie's chest as she gave the girl a short goodbye wave. A moment later they were gone.

"One day you're going to have to show me that trick," Ben said, sidling up next to her. He held an old blue bandanna to the bleeding wound at his temple where his head had struck the mirror.

"Does that mean you're admitting that you're wrong?" Charlie asked. "That it's actually good to have me along?"

Ben shook his head and a mischievous grin stretched his lips. "Now, let's not get crazy."

Charlie chuckled. "You're going to find me indispensable. I know it."

Ben rolled his eyes. "So where do we find this Layla Blake?"

Charlie turned to Jason. "She's a high school student. You think you can help us with that?"

"Yeah," Jason said. "Let's go back to the station and we'll do a search. If she's got a driver's license, we'll find her."

"Great. Lead the way." Charlie nodded and followed him down the steps.

CHAPTER 13

J ason turned into the gated community of Frawley's Landing on the Stono River. A security guard came out of a guard shack styled like a mini Acadian mansion made of white clapboard and vintage bricks. Jason flashed his badge and told the security guard that he needed to go to Layla Blake's address. The guard complied, waving them through.

"Well that was easier than I expected," Jason said as he rolled up his window and drove into the development.

"You're welcome," Ben said from the back seat. He had left his motorcycle at the sheriff's station and opted to ride along with them.

"What did you do?" Charlie asked, twisting in her seat and throwing him a dirty look.

"I just made him want to comply with us, that's all," Ben said. "It's not as if I'm trying to control his life. I just helped him to make the right decision that's all."

"Well that's an interesting trick," Jason said.

"It's also gray magic," Charlie said. "I would expect more out of a Defender of Light."

"Well technically I'm not a Defender of Light. Since that's really the Council of Seven. I just work for them and they give me a certain amount of leeway to do my work."

"So you're really a hired gun, is that what you're saying?"

"No, not exactly. I'm a highly trained agent. But we are allowed to use gray magic up to a point."

Charlie scowled. "Well that's not Machiavellian at all, is it? The ends justifying the means."

"No, it's all right," Jason chimed in. "It's not unlike what we do when we interview people. We don't always tell the truth. Sometimes we out-and-out lie to people to get them to tell us what we want."

"You're splitting hairs. And I don't always agree with that tactic, either." Charlie folded her arms and turned forward again in her seat.

"Well, if it gets us in to see Layla Blake, then I'm all for it," Jason said, taking a right onto Heron Drive.

"I like this guy," Ben said. Charlie shook her head

and rolled her eyes while staring at the mini-mansions they passed heading for Layla's address

"This is a pretty fancy neighborhood for a kid into witchcraft," Ben said.

"It's probably a form of rebellion," Charlie said. "There's a lot of pressure on the kids in this town to be cheerleaders and football players. Not everybody wants to conform to that. And if you want to rebel, what better way to do it than witchcraft? That is the ultimate shock in a town like this."

"Really? I didn't get that uptight sort of vibe from this place," Ben said. "Being so close to the beach and all."

"Actually, it's Charleston's influence. It's a lot more liberal than most places in the state. There's a lot of transience around here because it's basically a beach town. But that doesn't mean we don't have our conservatives. When my cousin Jen opened The Kitchen Witch Café it was a huge deal when she put witch in the name."

"Of course it was," Ben said shaking his head.

"We're here," Jason said as he pulled into the driveway of a massive Mediterranean-styled house with two curved staircases leading from the large front porch to the brick lined driveway. He parked behind a BMW SUV and turned so he could look at both Charlie and Ben.

"All right," Jason started. "Since I'm about to use

my badge to get into that house, y'all have to play by my rules. Any questions?"

"None for me," Charlie said. "Is it all right, though, if I ask questions?"

"Have I ever been able to stop you?" Jason said, half a grin curving his lips.

"Point taken," Charlie said. She twisted in her seat again so she could look at Ben. "I don't think you should do any of your little mind control tricks."

"That's what *he's* going to do." Ben frowned and sounded defensive. "He's just going to do it with language."

"Yeah, well, it's his investigation," Charlie said. "We're just along for the ride."

"Fine," Ben said.

Jason pulled his key fob out of the ignition, ending the back and forth before he got any more heated. "Okay, let's go."

The three of them got out of the car and headed up the steps. Jason pulled his badge from his front pocket and rang the doorbell.

A few moments later the heavy, carved door opened, and Melinda Helms stood there with a strange smile on her face.

"Oh my goodness, Charlie Payne. Is that you?"

Jason and Ben both turned and stared at Charlie.

"Well hey, Melinda," Charlie said, her cheeks

190

flooding with heat. "I didn't realize this was your house."

"Oh, you know Josh. He always dreamed of the big house on the river. So here we are."

"Yes indeed, here we are," Charlie said, forcing a smile. All she could think about was what Lisa said at dinner the other night that Josh and Melinda had separated.

Jason cleared his throat and flashed his badge. "Well, we're sorry to intrude ma'am but we're looking for someone who has a registered driver's license at this address."

Melinda's strange smile widened. "Oh?" she said, her voice going up an octave. "Who are you with again?"

"My name is Deputy Jason Tate and I'm with the sheriff's department." Jason held his badge out for her.

"Oh." Melinda sounded taken aback. She examined the badge closely. "And who are you looking for?"

"Layla Blake," Jason said.

"What has that girl done now?" Melinda's smile faded, and her lips pressed into a straight line. She took a step back and gestured for them to enter. Jason stepped in first followed by Charlie and then Ben. "What's this about? Why do you need to talk to Layla?"

"I can't really comment on a case, but Layla's name came up during our investigation. I need to ask some routine questions that's all. Are you Layla's mother?"

"No, of course not. Do I look old enough to have a sixteen-year-old? She's my niece. My sister's not well, and she's been living with us since December," Melinda said. "Do I need to call my lawyer?"

"Well that would be up to you ma'am, but just know that means we need to take Layla down to the station for formal questioning if you go that route," Jason said.

Melinda's gaze darted between Jason and Charlie as if she were trying to figure out why Charlie was with the deputy. She scowled. "Wait right here and I'll go get her."

Melinda headed up the curved staircase to the second floor. Once on the landing, she disappeared down a long hallway.

Charlie took in the foyer with its marble floor and pale gray walls that stretched to a twenty-foot ceiling. An intricately detailed crystal chandelier hung from the ceiling. Two sets of double doors flanked the foyer. On the left was a formal living room, filled with expensive antiques and furniture upholstered in dark blue velvet and silver brocade. On the right was a formal dining room with a table that could seat twelve and a large brick fireplace on the far wall.

"Looks like Melinda's doing pretty well for herself," Charlie said softly.

"You know her?" Jason asked.

"Yeah, we went to high school together," Charlie said.

"This really is a small town," Ben muttered.

"You have no idea," Charlie said.

Melinda appeared at the top of the steps accompanying a tall, slim teenage girl with spiky black hair. She wore diamond patterned black stockings beneath a black tulle skirt and a black form-fitting cami-top with a sheer black blouse over it. A black velvet choker accentuated her pale, slim neck. The girl's blue eyes were rimmed in thick black eyeliner and Charlie thought her bored expression and lack of conformity must have driven someone like Melinda insane.

"Ma'am, would you mind if we spoke with Layla alone?" Jason asked.

"Well, I don't know about that. I'm her guardian I should probably be here," Melinda said.

"It's fine, Aunt Melinda," Layla said. "I swear I haven't done anything, so I don't mind answering their questions."

"Well if you're sure," Melinda said.

"I am." Layla nodded and gave her aunt a reassuring smile.

"All right then, can I get y'all some iced tea?" Melinda said.

"That would great," Jason said. "Thank you."

"I'm gonna check on Camille and then I'll get your refreshments," Melinda said. She gave her niece a pointed look before she returned upstairs. As soon as she was out of sight, Layla folded her arms across her chest and scowled at Jason.

"Whatever it is, I didn't do it. I have been to school and home," Layla said defensively.

Jason stepped back. "Charlie, this is your show."

"Layla, my name is Charlie Payne, and I had a conversation with a friend of yours tonight."

Layla shifted her gaze to Charlie, looking down her nose. "I don't really have any friends."

"So you weren't friends with Ryan Whisnant?"

Layla shrugged. "I know her, but I wouldn't exactly call us friends. Why? What did she say about me?"

"Well, she said that you were a little weird and into witchcraft."

"That bitch," Layla muttered under her breath. She gritted her teeth and shook her head.

"So which is more offensive to you?" Charlie asked. "The fact she called you weird? Or because she told us about your spell work?"

Layla's gaze darted to the top of the stairs. She

lowered her voice. "I don't know what you're talking about."

"I think you do," Charlie said.

"Listen, Layla ..." Jason pulled a photo from his back pocket and looked down at it thoughtfully. "Did you see Ryan at school today?"

"No," she said. "I think her stepfather died recently and I know she's missed several days because of it."

"I want you to take a look at this," Jason said handing her the photograph.

Layla took the photo and studied it for a moment. Her pale face took on a gray hue and her breath became shallow as she looked down at the crime scene photo of Ryan's body crumpled at the bottom of the steps. "My God. What happened to her?"

"Her neck was broken. I'm investigating her death," Jason said. "And sometimes I call Charlie into help in very special cases."

Layla looked up from the picture. "You don't think I did this, do you?"

"No, Layla, we know who did it," Charlie said. "Ryan told me."

"I thought you'd said Ryan was dead," Layla said, her eyes full of confusion.

"She is dead," Charlie said. "That's my specialty. I can talk to the dead. And I had a conversation with Ryan this evening. Which is why we're here."

Layla laughed. "This is some sort of joke?"

"Come on Layla," Ben said. "You know it's not a joke. If I go upstairs and I look under the floorboard that you have dug out in your bedroom, I'm going to find a spell book. Right? Probably Boorman's Everyday Spell Work. Or A Caster's Guide to a Charmed Life by Gilstrap. If I search a little deeper, I may even find a family grimoire."

The smile on Layla's face faded, and she swallowed hard. "How do you know that?"

"Because I'm a witch," he said. "Just like you are."

Layla's lips twisted into a frown. "What do you want from me?"

"We need to know about the curse that you gave Ryan and the curse that you cast on Debra Duguid," Charlie said.

"What are you talking about? Who is Debra Duguid?" Layla asked.

"She's the mayor's wife," Jason said.

"Listen, I didn't give anybody other than Ryan a curse and it wasn't to kill anybody. The only thing I did was have her concentrate on what she wanted. I figured she must have wanted him dead."

"She says she didn't," Charlie said.

"We'll she's lying," Layla said. "I mean he used to beat the crap out of her. Seriously, she came to school with bruises on her body all the time."

"And no one did anything about that?" Jason asked.

"Not that I know of. But I haven't been there very long. I don't think the teachers even noticed though."

"But you did," Jason said.

"Yeah, sure. I found her crying in the bathroom a couple weeks ago because she didn't want to go to gym. She had run out of excuses as to why she couldn't change, and she was afraid somebody would see the big ass bruise on her back that son of a bitch gave her when he threw her into a wall."

"Yes, I'm familiar with her stepfather's temper," Charlie said. "Well if you didn't cast the curse on Debra Duguid, who did?"

Layla shrugged. "I don't know. Are you going to arrest me?"

Jason shook his head. "No. There are no laws against cursing someone, at least none I can enforce."

Layla let out a nervous laugh. "Thank god."

"Not so fast," Ben said. "You still have to be held accountable. Death curses are a serious matter to the Defenders of Light."

"Who are the Defenders of Light?" Layla asked warily.

"They're the judge, jury and executioner of the magical world," Ben said.

"Stop scaring her," Charlie said.

"She should be scared. Her actions caused a

death, regardless of her intentions. If that happened in Jason's world, she would be charged with involuntary manslaughter and even possibly serve jail time," Ben said.

"He's right. If I had a law that allowed me to enforce consequences for casting a curse and a prosecutor could prove that her actions resulted in a death, it's very possible she'd spend time in jail." Jason put his hands on his hips and nodded. Charlie wasn't sure if this was some sort of good cop/bad cop routine. "I know you didn't mean to, but you did admit that you're at least partly responsible, Layla."

"I'm not even seventeen yet. I don't want to go to jail." Layla took a step back, panic filling her pretty face. "Maybe I should get my aunt down here."

"Just calm down, nobody's sending you to jail." Ben held his hands up. "But what I will have to do is issue you a warning."

"Okay." Layla's brow furrowed as she listened to Ben. "Is that all?"

"No." Ben shoved his hand in the front pocket of his pants and pulled something out. He opened his fingers and quickly blew a silvery powder into Layla's face. The girl breathed it in and then began to cough.

"What the hell?" Charlie said, stepping between Ben and the girl. "What was that?"

"It's a monitoring spell," Ben said. "Layla Blake,

you have been found guilty of executing a death curse and for next twelve moon's the Defenders of Light will be monitoring every spell you craft. If you continue to practice the dark arts, then you may be brought before the Council of Seven for further judgment and punishment. Do you understand the charges against you?"

"I didn't know." Layla covered her mouth, her large blue eyes watery.

"You didn't know that purposefully causing a death is wrong?" Ben asked, his tone hard and unforgiving.

Fat tears pushed onto Layla's face and her black makeup streaked across her cheeks. "I didn't know it was illegal."

"Magic is more than just spells and potions," Ben said. "It is also about intention and will, and recognizing that there is an equilibrium that must be maintained. When you play with dark forces without thinking about the consequences, it can throw the world completely out of balance."

"I didn't mean for anyone to die." Layla's lips quivered as she spoke.

"I know. But someone did die," Ben said. "I'll be keeping an eye on your magical movements. If you stay away from dark magic, then I'll be back to remove the spell."

"What happens if she doesn't," Charlie asked.

"Then I'll have no choice but to take her before the Council. Then her fate will be up to them. If they decide to go easy on her, all they may do is bind her magic so that she never accesses it again."

"And if they don't go easy on her?" Jason asked.

"If she causes another death? She could pay with her life."

Layla burst into tears and Charlie put her arm around the girl's shoulders. "It won't come to that. Do you hear me?" Charlie whispered into the girl's ears. "I won't let it, and neither will you."

CHAPTER 14

Debra's funeral was set for 11 AM on Tuesday at the Third Street Methodist Church. Jen watched as her sister parked her little white BMW on the street in front of the Kitchen Witch Café and hop out. Lisa wore a smart, black suit paired with a pale yellow blouse and a pair of black pumps that Jen thought defied reason. When did five-inch heels become the norm? Jen untied her apron, slipped it over her head, and folded it neatly before stowing it in the cubby beneath the cash register. She wore a white blouse with small gray daisies, a black cardigan, her best black trousers and a pair of black flats.

"Is that what you're wearing?" Lisa asked.

Jen ran her fingers through her hair trying to tame

the short waves. "Yes," Jen said, taking in her sister's perfect French twist. "Is that what you're wearing?"

"Yes. Why?"

"You look like a lawyer," Jen smirked. "It might scare people."

"Well, I am a lawyer and I'm okay with being scary." Lisa smiled. "You on the other hand look like a soccer mom."

"I'd rather not be scary," Jen said. She grabbed the two brown paper bags from the counter. "Let's get going."

"Wait. Is Charlie riding with us?" Lisa looked at her watch.

"No, she said she'd meet us there," Jen said.

"Is Daphne coming?"

"I have no idea, she didn't say," Jen said.

"What's that?" Lisa pointed to the paper bags.

"It's food," Jen said. "For the reception."

Lisa frowned. "Reception?"

"Yeah, we have to go to the reception."

"Why?" Lisa asked. "Isn't the funeral bad enough?"

"I just thought it might be nice to pay our respects," Jen said as the two made their way toward Lisa's car.

"Isn't that what the funeral's for?" Lisa sounded dubious.

"Well, I wouldn't want people to say we're unsupportive." Jen opened the door and put the bags on the floorboard and sat down. She really hated this car. The seats were slung too low, and she always felt like she was climbing inside the cockpit a race car. Of course with the way Lisa drove she almost wished it had the harness of a racing car. She settled her legs around the bags and strapped herself in.

Lisa shrugged. "Okay. Whatever you say." She cast a look at Jen and fastened her seatbelt. "It couldn't be at all that you're just as nosy as old Debra. You're just nicer and more discreet, which is why nobody calls you on it."

"Obviously you don't have a problem doing it." Jen folded her arms across her chest. Her sister was right to question her motives for wanting to go to the reception. Jen would have never admitted it out loud, but she wanted to see if Josh Helms showed up to support Kristen and validate her theory that he was the secret beau.

"Nope," Lisa grinned. "None at all."

When they arrived at the church, a crowd of people had already gathered waiting to get inside.

"I had no idea she was so popular," Jen said.

"The way I see it, she's got two things going for her. One, she's the mayor's wife, and two, most of these people are here to make sure the Wicked Witch of the East is really dead," Lisa said.

"That's an awful thing to say," Jen said.

Lisa shrugged. "It is, but it doesn't make it any less true."

It took several minutes before they could get inside. Jen stood on her toes scanning the rows closer to the front for empty seats. Lisa grabbed her arm and leaned in close. "Let's sit in the back."

"No, we should sit near Kristen," Jen said. "The whole reason I'm here is to support her."

"We're never going to get near her and if we sit in the back, we'll be able to see who comes in better," Lisa said.

"Good point," Jen said. Lisa led them to the very back row, and they sat down on the side closest to the door. Jen started making mental notes, especially about the women coming in to the church.

"Hey y'all," a voice said from Jen's right. She turned to find her cousin Daphne plopping down next to her.

"Well, hey," Jen said. "I wasn't sure if you were gonna make it or not.

"Debra Duguid was one of my best customers. There's no way I'd miss her funeral," Daphne said. "I just wish Tom would've let me do her hair."

"Did you ask?" Jen said.

"I did, but he pays Mandy Pogue from Fancy Klips to do make-up and hair." Daphne twirled the blunt end of her pink-tipped hair around her finger. "I'm surprised to see you here Lisa."

"Yeah, well Jen dragged me here and I'm nosy," Lisa said, smirking.

"Is Charlie coming?" Daphne asked, craning her neck looking around.

"She said she was, but she had to do something first. You know funerals aren't her favorite thing because ... well you know."

"Yeah. It'd be interesting if Debra showed up, though, wouldn't it?" Daphne chuckled.

"Shush," Jen said pointing to Kristen as she made her way toward the back pew.

"Hey, Jen. Hey, Lisa. It's so nice of y'all to come," Kristen said. "Hi Daphne. My mother just loved you."

"Aw, that is so sweet. Well, she was definitely one of my favorite customers. I'm so sorry she's not with us anymore," Daphne said.

Kristen's eyes became teary and she sniffled into a white cotton handkerchief. "Thank you all for coming. I've got to get back. Now." Kristen said jerking her thumb toward the front of the chapel.

"We'll talk to you later," Jen said.

She watched Kristen make her way back toward the front pew where her father and brother Todd sat.

"Hey y'all," Charlie said, sliding into the pew next to Lisa.

"Billy at 10 o'clock," Jen whispered in Lisa's ear. Her sister grimaced.

"Hello, ladies," Billy said, straightening his tie. "Do you have room for me?"

Jen and Lisa spoke at the same time echoing different sentiments.

"Of course," Jen said.

"No," Lisa said, her mouth a straight line.

Jen's cheeks heated with embarrassment.

"Hey, Billy," Charlie said. "You can sit by me." Charlie scooted, forcing Lisa, Jen and Daphne to move down the pew.

Jen felt her sister's body tense. Lisa stared straight ahead, not looking at Charlie or Billy as he took a seat.

"Well that's interesting," Lisa muttered as she watched Josh Helms take a seat behind Kristen. He leaned forward put his hand on Kristen's shoulder and gave it a very visible squeeze. Lisa leaned close to Jen's ear. "Is that what you were waiting for?"

"Yep." Jen nodded. Her eyes scanned the other pews. There didn't seem to be any sign of Melinda. Jen's breath caught in her throat when Ben Sutton walked in looking handsome as ever wearing a dark gray blazer over a white button-down and a pair of jeans. He stopped at the end of the pew and looked at down at Charlie and smiled.

"Any room for me?" Ben asked. He glanced into Jen's face. Her cheeks heated when their eyes met.

"Sure. Billy, would you mind switching places with ..." Charlie started.

Lisa grabbed her cousin's wrist, squeezing it tight.

"Ow." Jen and Lisa both threw a questioning look at Charlie. "What?"

"No," Lisa mouthed.

Charlie scowled and whispered harshly, "Stop it. I'm not moving if that's what you're worried about."

Music began to play indicating the service would begin soon. Billy scooted toward Charlie forcing everyone to move down so Ben could take a seat on the end of the pew.

"Good morning," the minister began. "We are here today to honor our sister in Christ, Debra Duguid."

Lisa relaxed a little and sat farther back in the pew. Jen glanced down the row at Ben. He was not paying attention as the minister droned on and on about what a valued citizen Debra was. Ben seemed to be scanning the crowd. Jen swept her gaze across the sanctuary. What was he looking for? Or maybe a better question was ... who?

Jen saw Charlie stiffen in her seat and lean forward. The temperature of the room dropped despite all the warm bodies and then the overhead lights flickered. A soft murmur spread through the church and Ben stood up and slipped out of the sanctuary.

"Sorry, Lisa," Charlie said softly just before she rose from the pew and followed him. A moment later two bulbs exploded raining slivers of white glass onto the crowd below and the rest of the room went dark.

CHAPTER 15

When Debra Duguid marched into the sanctuary and began to tell off her husband Charlie knew she was dealing with an unpredictable spirit. When the lights started to explode, she shifted to being dangerous. As the security lights flickered on, Charlie slipped out of the sanctuary to find Ben. They needed a plan and fast, only this time she didn't have a God's-eye cross with her to trap the spirit. She would have to do something she hated thinking about. She would have to rely on Ben to trap the spirit. But first she needed to talk to the dead woman.

"Charlie?" a familiar voice said. Charlie turned to find Tom approaching.

"What are you doing here?" she asked.

"I'm the funeral director. Remember?"

"Right," Charlie said, shaking her head. "By the way, Deborah Duguid just walked into the sanctuary and blew out the lights."

"All right," Tom said. "I'll have to go change and capture her."

"No, wait I need to talk to her," Charlie said.

"About what?" Tom asked.

"I need to understand exactly how she died," Charlie said. "It's important."

Shouting came from inside the sanctuary and the door flew open and mourners with panic written all over their faces began to flood out.

"I'll see what I can do," Tom said. "Right now, I need to talk to the minister so that we can get this mess under control."

"Fine. I'll see if I can find her," Charlie said. She pushed her way through the crowd to the stairway on the side of the lobby leading to the upper balcony seats overlooking the sanctuary. Once upstairs, she approached the railing to get a better view of the darkened church. The last of the attendees had left and only Tom and the minister remained in the middle of the long aisle up to the pulpit. The only light coming in was from tall windows on each side of the building and a large abstract stained-glass window behind the pulpit. The church had lost the original window in Hurricane Hugo almost 30 years ago. The purples and reds and yellows and blues of

old. Charlie scanned the sanctuary for any sign of
Debra's spirit but there was no shadow, no flicker, no
odd light to indicate her presence. Still the sanctuary
remained cold. Charlie listened as Tom and the
funeral director decided to move the casket and
finish the service at the graveside. Perhaps Charlie
would have luck finding Debra in the cemetery
behind the church.

As she contemplated all this, like an unexpected
shock of cold water to the face, suddenly the hair on
the back of her neck stood up. Charlie inhaled a deep
breath, listened for a sign. Had someone opened a
window? A hidden hole in the roof allowed in a rush
of icy wind? Her heartbeat ramped up, her brain's
code for danger. Charlie never lied to herself; she
knew what it was.

Slowly she turned and found herself face to face
with the spirit of Debra Duguid.

"I know you," Debra said. "You're Evangeline
Ferrebe's niece, aren't you?"

In life Debra Duguid had been intimidating. In
the early seventies, she'd been a beauty queen and
she never let anyone forget it. Even at sixty she left
home perfectly coiffed, eyes made up, and dressed to
the nines. Charlie could never remember the woman
without her signature pink lips.

211

In death Debra had transformed to something altogether different. She emanated a dark energy. Anger and sadness rolled off of her in waves and crashed over Charlie, making her nauseous. Charlie swallowed back the sour taste that filled her mouth.

"Yes, I am," Charlie said.

"We were rivals when we were young," Debra said. "Martin chased her, and I chased Martin. I thought for sure he was gonna be in love with Evangeline forever. But she was such a tease. Then she met Ronnie Ferrebe, and that was that. Martin turned to me for comfort, and I got the life I wanted."

Debra's face darkened. "I was not ready to die."

"I know," Charlie said. "None of us want to go, Ms. Duguid. But they're still good things that could happen to you."

"I thought there would be a light or tunnel or something. But it's just been torture instead. All the things." Debra said. "You know all the things, good and bad." Her lips quivered and if Debra could have shed tears, Charlie knew she would have.

"I know," Charlie said. "I know. That can still happen. But before it does Before you leave for the next world. I need to know more about the day you died."

Debra glided backwards, her hand drifting up to her throat. "I don't want to remember."

"I know this is painful and I'm so sorry, but

someone cursed you. That's why you died, and I need find that person, so I can stop them from ever doing it again. Please, Ms. Duguid. If you help me, I will make sure you see that light."

A loud keening sound resonated, making Charlie's ears ache and her teeth hum. She clapped her hands over her ears to stop the sound, but it didn't help. It was as if the sound was coming from inside her head. Debra continued to wail, and the sound swirled around Charlie's head. She swayed with dizziness.

The hymnals that had been laid out on the pews began to fly across the balcony, landing on the seats below. Charlie tried to duck but one of the hymnals struck her in the side of her head, knocking her off balance. Her hip hit the old wooden balcony, and it shimmied and creaked against her weight.

"You there!" The minister called. "Stop that right now." A hymnal sailed over the railing and he dove out of the way just in time to avoid being hit. The book landed on the back of one of the benches, its cover ripping away from the delicate yellowed paper of the old book. Another hymnal struck Charlie in the shoulder and she swiped out at it. She quickly ducked down behind the long, polished benches next to the railing. For a brief second, she wished she still had her pentacle to protect her.

"Ms. Duguid," Charlie said. "Please, stop. Talk to me. Let me help you."

A loud cracking sound thundered through the sanctuary. And the pew Charlie was hiding behind lifted into the air. And hovered over her head. Charlie stared at the long wooden bench, paralyzed. Thinking of the words Debra had said to her. I was not ready to die.

"Hey, Debra." Ben's voice boomed across the balcony. "Put that bench down."

His words broke Charlie's paralysis, and she scrambled from beneath the bench just as Debra dropped it onto the floor. It cracked down the center and sagged. Ben pulled something from his pocket and tossed it at Debra's apparition. The old woman screamed and disappeared.

Ben was kneeling next to Charlie a moment later. "Are you okay?"

Charlie was almost touched by the concern in his face. "Yeah, I'm fine." She touched the tender skin around the growing goose egg on the side of her head. "Was that salt?"

"Yeah," he said. "I usually keep some on me. We should probably get you some, too. And maybe some sort of protection pendant."

"I think that's a great idea," Charlie said. Ben got to his feet and helped Charlie to hers.

"Looks like we may have lost her for now," Ben

said. "Were you able to get any information out of her?"

"Nothing that really made sense. She seems to be doing nothing except thinking about the past and she said that she had seen it all. I'm not sure what that meant."

"I'm no expert on spirits. But there are some cultures that believe that when you die, you have all the knowledge in the world. At your fingertips, so to speak. You know every thought that people had about you and you know every deed and misdeed you did and that people did to you. Maybe she's seen something that's devastated her."

"Her husband is supposedly having an affair," Charlie said. "His daughter knew but I don't think his wife did."

"Well my guess is she knows now," Ben said.

"She's pissed and sad," Charlie said. "Her emotions made me physically sick. I thought I was going to throw up."

"Where would you go? If you just learned everything you believed about your world was a lie?" Ben asked.

"I would probably go and confront the person at the heart of the lie," Charlie said.

"Exactly," Ben said. "And where would that be?"

"Home," Charlie said. "I bet you Debra went home."

CHAPTER 16

Charlie and Ben joined the small crowd standing around Debra's grave. After the strange happenings, half of the parking lot had cleared out. Only her cousins and Debra's closest friends and family remained. Charlie observed the way the minister held his Bible tightly against his chest as he spoke about Debra and what a pillar of the community she was. She also noticed Josh Helms standing next to Kristin holding her hand. Charlie scanned the cemetery for any sign of Debra. But the woman's spirit didn't reappear. Jen moved through the crowd and sidled up next to Charlie.

"Are you all right?" Jen whispered.

"Yeah," Charlie nodded. "I'm okay. Debra's not though. She got a little upset." Charlie turned her head so her cousin could see the faint blue bruise at her temple.

"Stars above," Jen said softly.

"Yes, she made a mess in the balcony. I wasn't too keen to go to the reception but now I need to go," Charlie said

"Okay," Jen said. "What about Ben?" Jen mouthed his name.

"Jury still out but I may have been wrong about him," Charlie said. Ben leaned forward and gave Jen a smile and a little wave. She bristled and shifted her gaze forward.

When the minister finished, Tom stepped up in his best black suit. He took the electronic box that would lower the casket into the grave and pressed the button. Kristin laid her forehead against Josh's shoulder and he slipped his arm around her and let her cry against him. The electronics squealed as the casket got closer to the bottom of the grave. Tom looked into the chamber. He gave the minister an awkward smile and pressed the button again. A moment later a loud crash jolted the assembled as Debra's casket dropped the last two feet. The crowd backed away from the grave and the minister gave Tom a mortified look.

"I'm so sorry," Tom said. "I've never had anything like this happen before."

"She's here somewhere," Charlie whispered into Ben's ear.

He nodded. "Let's see what she does."

Charlie continued to look around, hoping to see Debra's spirit reappear. What caught her eye was a blue dress. Charlie squinted her eyes trying to figure out if it was a real woman or an apparition standing in the shadow of the woods at the edge of the cemetery. She nudged Jen with her elbow.

"Do you see her?" she whispered. "Under the oak trees over near the fence."

"That's Melinda Helms," Jen said.

"Why is she standing over there?" Charlie asked.

"Why do you think? Her husband has his arm around another woman. Separated or not, it's still humiliating," Jen said.

"Yeah, exactly. Melinda's never been one to wallow in humiliation," Charlie said.

"Well she's also never ended a marriage. People do all kinds of things when relationships end," Jen said.

"Yes, they do," Charlie said.

The minister asked everyone to bow their heads, and he said a quick prayer for the peaceful rest of Debra Duguid's soul. The crowd dispersed, and Charlie glanced over her shoulder one last time at the woods where Melinda Helms had stood. A cold finger touched her heart sending a shiver through her. Melinda was gone.

Once they got to the parking lot Charlie and Jen went their separate ways. Ben trailed behind Charlie.

"You want to ride with me or you want to follow me?" Charlie asked.

"I'll drive my bike, thanks," Ben said.

"Okay, have it your way. I may be a few minutes late though. I need to stop at The Pig and get some salt."

"Good idea," Ben chuckled. "I'll keep my eye out for Debra to get there."

"That's fine. But whatever you do, don't put her in that amulet of yours. I need to talk to her."

"No problem. I can't put the second spirit into it anyway, not until I've cleared out the spirit of Tony Smoak. I need to talk about it with that reaper friend of yours and see if he can help me out with that."

"Good idea," Charlie said as she unlocked her car and got in. Ben climbed onto his motorcycle and adjusted his gear. He drove away as she fastened her seatbelt and watched Josh and Kristen walk across the parking lot. A large black SUV pulled out of a parking space and sped past them. Horns blared as it turned onto the road without slowing down for the oncoming traffic.

CHAPTER 17

The ride to the mayor's house was quiet and Charlie savored her alone time. On the seat next to her was a paper bag with two large cartons of salt inside. Just in case. She turned into the mayor's neighborhood admiring the perfectly manicured lawns of St. Augustine grass. The azaleas had faded by mid-April but there were still neat little rows of daffodils standing guard around the bases of flowerbeds and trees. It wouldn't be long before the heat made them fade, too, and summer annuals like mounding petunias would replace them. She glanced toward the blur of perfectly landscaped yards. She took a curve around a large pond and began to see the cars parked along the side of the road.

"I didn't mean to get so upset," a voice said from her back seat. It startled Charlie so badly she slammed on the brakes leaving a trail of black on the asphalt and the acrid scent of burning rubber stung her nose. Charlie glanced into the rearview mirror and she realized she still had not spirit-proofed her car. Her hand flew to her chest.

"You scared the crap out of me, Ms. Duguid," Charlie snapped without thinking.

"I apologize. It's just very overwhelming to realize that you're dead," Debra said. Charlie pulled her car over to the side of the road and put it in park. She turned and stared at the spirit sitting in her back seat. Debra fiddled with the pearls around her neck. A habit she must've had in life.

"I imagine it is," Charlie said. "You said something about seeing everything. What did you mean by that?"

"Exactly the way it sounds. Everything seems to just open up and you know things about people. Private things," she said, her voice filled with sadness. "I don't think we were meant to know these things. I certainly didn't want to."

"What do you know?" Charlie asked.

"It doesn't matter now. I'm dead and there's nothing I can do about it."

"That's not quite true," Charlie said. "There are things you can do. Things that will help you deal with this new knowledge I think."

"Please," Debra said, sounding a little desperate. "I'll do anything if it will make this stop."

"Tell me about the day you died. Do you remember what happened?"

Debra's lips curved into a smile but there was nothing warm or inviting about it. Instead it made Charlie's heart ache.

"Yes, I remember. For the first time in fifteen years I got flowers from my husband."

* * *

WHEN DEBRA FINISHED HER STORY, HER CHEST expanded as if she was taking a deep breath. "How amazing," she muttered. "There's a light."

Charlie nodded her head. "You should go toward it."

"It's so bright," Debra said. "It's like looking at the sun but without being burned."

Charlie opened her mouth to encourage Debra again, but the spirit disappeared before she could. "Rest in peace, Debra."

Charlie tucked one of the cartons of salt into her purse, got out of the car and walked up the street toward the mayor's house. As she drew closer, she saw Ben leaning against one of the brick posts on the side of the driveway. "What took you so long?"

"I had to stop for supplies," she said. She opened her bag, so he could see the round blue carton.

"Very good," he said.

"I had a visitor on my way over."

"Who?" Ben asked as they made their way up the driveway to the large antebellum house overlooking the river.

"Debra Duguid. She's moved on by the way. So there won't be any need to trap her."

"What did she say?"

"She said that the day she died she received flowers and inside the flowers was a box with a bracelet made from onyx and gold beads," Charlie said.

"A classic cursed object. A piece of jewelry," Ben said.

"Yep," Charlie said. "That's exactly what I thought. My question, though, is, was it really for Debra?"

"Why wouldn't it be? Was there a card?" Ben asked.

"No. No card. It was delivered to the pharmacy," Charlie said.

Ben stopped and stared at her, shaking his head. "Why does that mean anything?"

"Duguid's pharmacy? Kristin's the pharmacist and Debra is the office manager. It's a family business. Martin Duguid was a pharmacist before he became mayor. Maybe the flowers weren't for Debra. Maybe they were for Kristin."

"Who is Kristin again?"

"She is Debra Duguid's daughter. She's also dating, if you want to call it that, Josh Helms. Melinda Helms soon to be ex-husband."

"Are you telling me this is about an affair?"

"Maybe. I'm thinking that Layla didn't tell us the truth. Maybe she did make a second curse. Maybe she saw her aunt in pain and wanted to do something for her," Charlie said.

"So she sent flowers to her uncle's mistress along with a cursed piece of jewelry. That is a very interesting theory." A grin stretched Ben's lips. "Sounds like we need to talk to Layla again."

"Actually, I think we should talk to Josh," Charlie said.

"Why?" Ben asked.

"Because he knows Melinda and Layla and has no reason to lie to us," Charlie said.

Ben nodded. "Okay. Let's go talk to Josh."

CHAPTER 18

C harlie found Jen fussing over the food. She watched a moment as her cousin added more paper plates and plastic forks to the end of the serving table.

"Why are you doing this?" Charlie asked as she approached her cousin. "You do not always have to be the one who takes care of the food."

Jen looked up at her and frowned. "I like taking care the food. I'm good at it. And it makes me feel helpful. How are you? How's your head?"

"Head hurts but I'm good," Charlie said before lowering her voice. "I talked to Debra. She's moved on and she gave me a lead."

Jen leaned in and whispered, "What kind of lead?"

"I found out what happened the day she died.

She handled a bracelet that I think was cursed," Charlie said softly. "Feels like I haven't talked to you in a million years. Did I tell you about Layla Blake?"

"No. Who's Layla Blake?"

"Melinda Helms' niece and she's a witch." Charlie mouthed the last word.

"What?" Jen said. "Are you sure?"

"Yep. She admitted to cursing Tony Smoak. Ben had to put her on some sort of probation with the DOL," Charlie said under her breath. "I don't think, though, that she stopped with one curse."

"You think she cursed Debra on purpose?" Jen asked.

Charlie shrugged her shoulder. "Melinda's her aunt. I think it was actually meant for Kristin."

"And Debra got to the bracelet before Kristin did." Jen gasped and covered her mouth. "And it killed her."

"Yep." Charlie glanced around the crowded living room of the mayor's house. "Where's Lisa?"

"Oh, she got irritated and went back to work. And Daphne had to go, too. She had customers. I was hoping I could get a ride with you."

"Of course," Charlie said. "I'll drop you off. We're gonna talk to Josh and then probably head over to Melinda's to talk to Layla again."

Jen nodded and scrunched up her face. "Can I throw something out there?"

"What?" Charlie asked.

"This is probably going to sound crazy," Jen began. "But what if it wasn't Layla?"

"Who would it be then?"

"What if it was Melinda?" Jen said.

"I ... well ..." Charlie thought about what her cousin was saying, trying to reconcile it with what she knew. "I guess it's possible, but wouldn't we know if she was a witch?"

"No, not necessarily. There are lots of witches who are in the broom closet," Jen said.

"I mean Melinda is just so ... normal," Charlie said.

"Or ... she wants us to think she's normal. You have to admit, up till recently, she's led a pretty charmed life. Too charmed, if you get my drift." Jen's eyebrows went up.

"Yeah, but ..." Charlie twisted her lips. "It wouldn't have occurred to me... that she was a witch."

"Oh it's occurred to me that's she a witch," Jen said wryly. "Whether she can perform a spell or not remains to be seen. But you know, now that I think about it, it wouldn't surprise me at all."

Jen stiffened and cleared her throat. Charlie glanced over her shoulder and saw Ben approaching them.

"I found Josh," Ben said. "He's out back near the pool talking to Melinda."

"Are you kidding me?" Charlie said.

"Nope," Ben said. "Come on."

Charlie and Jen followed him through the crowd. A pair of French doors opened up to the back deck from the living room. It looked out over the kidney-shaped swimming pool and beyond back to the marsh and the Kiawah River. Charlie took a spot next to the deck railing so she could get a good view of Josh and Melinda Helms arguing on the side of the pool. Ben positioned himself in front of Charlie and Jen pushed close to Charlie's shoulder.

"What are you doing?" Charlie asked.

"What? This is better than when we used to watch soap operas in high school. I mean you can almost imagine what they're arguing about, right? Wouldn't you like to be a dragonfly sitting on one of those chaises?"

Ben shook his head. "Not really."

Jen bristled. Charlie pressed her elbow up against Jen's arm in solidarity.

"Let's just pretend that we're all talking and not watching them, okay?" Charlie said.

"Holy moly," Jen said under her breath. "Are you seeing this?"

Charlie glanced across the pool to see Melinda take Josh's hand and press it against her left breast over her heart. Josh's face went blank and Melinda's lips continued to move. "Is she—?"

"That's what it looks like," Jen said.

"Do you do this all the time?" Ben asked.

"What?" Jen said curtly.

"Talk in code," Ben said, sounding irritated.

"Yes," Charlie said flatly. She lowered her voice. "Now if you would pay attention, you would see that Melinda is casting a spell over him."

Ben turned his head and narrowed his eyes. "Looks like she's trying to influence him. Maybe a love spell?"

Josh blinked his eyes and shook his head. He tried to jerk his hand away and Melinda held onto it. At first it just seemed like a desperate move to Charlie. Until Melinda got angry and yanked his hand down and bent his fingers back. Josh jerked his hand back, his face a mask of pain. Melinda glanced around quickly to see who was looking at her and then took him by the tie and pulled his face down close to her ears. She uttered a few words and planted a kiss on his lips. Then let him go.

"You are crazy!" Josh said, cradling his hand to his chest. "I cannot wait until this year is over and I can divorce you," he yelled as he stormed away.

A soft murmur traveled across the different groups of people, all watching. Melinda scowled, her face red with embarrassment. She folded her arms and walked away.

"Holy crap," Jen said. "We can have our own soap opera. When the tide turns."

"You are mean, Jen Holloway," Charlie scolded.

"Not as mean as she is. I think she broke his fingers. Look." Jen jerked a thumb toward Kristin hovering over Josh's hand.

"I think she did more than that," Ben said.

A deep line formed between his brows and he started toward the couple. Josh suddenly became very pale, and he held his injured hand against his stomach and doubled over.

"Josh?" Kristin said, sounding panicked. He fell to his knees and began to heave. Blood splattered his lips, and he fell to the ground shaking, holding his stomach. "Oh my God. Someone call 911. Josh? Baby can you hear me?" Kirsten bent over him, tears streaming down her face.

Ben knelt next to Josh. "What happened?"

"I don't know. His wife broke his finger I think and then he started complaining about his stomach hurting. He was treated for an ulcer last year, but he's been on medication and he's been fine," Kristin blurted out in a rush.

"Stomach or duodenal?"

"Stomach," Kristin said. "Are you a doctor?"

"Something like that," Ben said. He turned Josh

onto his back. He glanced up searching the crowd. "Charlie, I need your help."

Charlie pushed through the circle of people that had moved in around Josh and Kristin. She knelt next to Ben. He leaned in close and whispered, "I just need you to focus on sending healing energy to him. Specifically, to his stomach."

"What are you going to do?" Charlie whispered. "This is too open for people to see."

"Don't worry about that. He could bleed out if we don't do something." Ben spoke softly, his eyes locking on hers. "You want that on your hands? Because I don't."

"All right," Charlie said. "I'll do my best but Jen's more experienced at this sort of thing than I am." Charlie peered into the faces of the onlookers but didn't find her cousin among them.

"Come on," Ben said. "We're wasting time."

Ben placed his hand over Josh's upper belly. "Put your hands around mine and focus."

Charlie did as she was told. She closed her eyes and listened as Ben began to chant something in Latin. It was unlike any spell she had ever heard. The warmth where her thumbs touched his pinkies grew to an almost unbearable heat but she couldn't pull away. Instead she focused on Ben's voice and its steady rhythm.

Josh began to moan and Charlie almost jerked her

hands away out of fear they were making him worse. But something about Ben's voice kept her hands in place. A moment later Josh stopped moaning and began to breathe easier. Ben sat back on his heels and took his hands away and Charlie followed his lead. "The worst is over for now, Josh. You still need to get checked out though."

"Josh? Are you all right sweetie?" Kristin asked, stroking Josh's face.

"The pain's gone. I don't know what you did but thank you," Josh said. Kristin helped him sit up then threw her arms around him and hugged him tight, crying.

"No problem," Ben said. He rose to his feet and pushed through the circle of people. Charlie jumped up and went after him.

"You just exposed us all," Charlie said.

"What I did was save his life. And thank you by the way. I don't think I could've done it without your energy." Ben threw a glance over his shoulder at the crowd around Josh and Kristin. "I wouldn't worry about it. They're not gonna remember it. It will all be a blur. They'll know something happened, they just won't remember the details."

"What was that spell you were chanting?" Charlie said. "I don't think I've ever seen anything like that."

"Well unless you study to be a healer you wouldn't have," he said.

Charlie touched his arm, stopping him in his tracks and stared at him. "I guess you're not as much of a tough guy as I thought you were."

He chuckled. "That's what you think of me? Well I guess I'm sorry to disappoint you."

"Not disappointed exactly. I guess I misjudged you. I'm sorry for that."

"Is that why Jen won't even look at me now without freezing me out?"

"Yeah," Charlie said. "That's my fault."

"Just for the record, I really do like her. I didn't ask her out because I was trying to get information," Ben said.

"Fair enough," Charlie said. "My cousins are the closest thing I have to sisters. I'm glad that you like her. She likes you too. I will say that if you hurt her, I will hunt you down and skin you alive."

"You use that kind of magic and you'd probably end up in front of the tribunal for murder," Ben said.

"Who said I would use magic? I would do it the old-fashioned way. And trust me, nobody would ever find your body," Charlie said with a wicked gleam in her eye.

Ben let out a nervous laugh. "Point taken. Come on, let's go find Jen and go hunt down Melinda."

A few minutes later the EMTs arrived and carted Josh Helms away in the back of an ambulance.

Once the hubbub had cleared, Charlie and Ben

WENDY WANG

began to look around for her cousin. They walked through the entire first floor of the mayor's house without finding Jen. As Charlie circled back around she asked several bystanders if they had seen Jen Holloway, but every one of them just shook their head no. She didn't start to panic until Ben met her in the middle of the living room with a worried look on his face.

"I didn't find her," Charlie said.

"There was a couple out on the front porch who said they saw Jen and Melinda get in her SUV and drive away," Ben said.

"Why would Jen go with Melinda?" Charlie asked.

"I don't know. The guy I was talking to said they looked like they were arguing," Ben said.

"That can't be good."

"No, I agree." Ben said. "My question is, did Jen go willingly or did Melinda somehow influence her?"

"Oh stars," Charlie said, panic squeezing her heart. "We need to find her. We need to find her now."

CHAPTER 19

Jen awoke with a headache and a stiff neck. She tried to move but found her arms tied behind her back and her feet tied to the legs of one of Melinda Helms's kitchen chairs. She glanced around the overly neat kitchen that looked like it belonged in a House and Gardens magazine. Under different circumstances she would've wanted to run her hands over the Italian marble counters and try her hand at baking some marvelous confection in one of the double ovens. Or maybe a simple sauté on the six-burner stove.

"Wakey, wakey," Melinda said as she entered the kitchen.

"How did I get here?" Jen asked. She struggled against the ropes binding her arms and legs.

"Well, you said that you wanted to discuss a few

things with me. Don't you remember?" Melinda said in a condescending tone.

Dizziness spun through Jen's head. "What did you do to me?"

"Just a little spell to subdue you and make you do what I want," Melinda said.

Jen fought to keep her head upright. She could feel Melinda's words boring into her brain like tentacles. "How long have you been a witch, Melinda?"

"All my life?" Melinda said shrugging. "I knew I was different when I was six years old. A lot like your Ruby. And my Grammy was a wonderful teacher. Unfortunately, she outlived her usefulness. Just like my parents and my sister."

Jen froze, unable to look away. "Sweet goddess, are you telling me you killed them all?"

"No. Of course not." Melinda frowned and shook her head. "Every single one of them died from a tragic accident or an unexpected illness."

"Is that what you're planning to do to me? You're gonna curse me, too?"

"No." Melinda exaggerated the word. "Of course not." She walked over to Jen and swept her bangs off her forehead. "You do what you're supposed to do and it won't come to that."

"I think I'll pass," Jen said.

Melinda laughed but there was no humor in it.

"Oh Jen. Jen. Jen. Jen. Do you know what my specialty is?"

Jen shook her head now.

"Ever since I was a small child, I have always been able to get people to see things my way and to believe the things that I want them to believe." Melinda pulled a chair from the kitchen table and set it down in front of Jen.

Jen settled her gaze on Melinda's face as her captor spoke. "You know, when we were in high school I was always jealous of you."

"Me? Why?" Jen said, incredulous.

"Because you didn't have to use magic to get people to like you. They just did.

"Melinda ...."

"Even now, all these years later people still really just like you. I mean, you're a respected business owner and a dutiful member of the community. After all this nonsense with Josh and Kristin is over and people have long forgotten about Debra Duguid and how she died, you and I are going to be best friends. You're going to make sure that people know what a wonderful person I am."

Melinda's eyes seemed to burrow into Jen's. "You're also going to get that friend of yours Ben to break that monitoring spell that he put on Layla."

"Are you kidding me?" Jen said. "Do you know how nuts you sound?"

"I'd be careful who you call nuts," Melinda warned.

"You are never going to get away with this. None of my family would believe me if I said 'oh Melinda Helms is my best friend and bosom buddy.' They would absolutely believe I was under some sort of spell," Jen said.

"Well then you will just have to work hard to convince them," Melinda said. "I think it will become your life's mission, actually."

"You're gonna have to kill me first because that ain't happening," Jen insisted.

"You really shouldn't joke about such things," Melinda said.

"Aunt Melinda?" Layla said from the kitchen doorway. The girl wore a worried expression. "Is everything all right?"

"Everything is just fine. Why don't you go check on Camille? Make sure she stays up in her room, then come down and help me with this spell. All right?"

"Aunt Melinda," Layla said her voice full of caution. "What if that man comes back? The one from the Defenders of Light? I mean they're monitoring me."

"Don't you worry about that," Melinda said. "My good friend Jen Holloway here is going to help us take care of that. Aren't you Jen?"

"Not a chance in hell," Jen said.

"Don't worry, you'll change your mind," Melinda said, patting Jen on the shoulder. She flashed an angry look at her niece. "Go on now. I said go check on Camille and get back down here."

Layla turned quickly and disappeared from the doorway.

The doorbell rang. Melinda shot a glance down the hall and scowled. "I'll be right back. Don't go anywhere."

As soon as Melinda left the kitchen Jen began to rock her chair backward and forward. She was almost up on her feet, but she didn't account for the heaviness of the chair and she overbalanced, falling forward. The chair fell onto its side carrying her with it. She banged her head on the floor and a dizziness swirled through her head. She squeezed her eyes shut until it passed and was able to get a better view of the rest of the kitchen. Melinda had tied her up in the dining nook. She had pulled the shades of the side windows, but Jen could see a French door leading to the back deck and yard. She saw his form peering into the windows of the back door and her heart soared at the sight of him. Through the glass she could see a glowing green plasma circling his hand as he twisted the brass door knob. She heard a click, and the door pushed open. Ben glanced around, then spotted her. He pulled a small box knife from his front pocket and knelt beside her.

"Oh my God," she whispered. "I am so glad to see you."

"I'm glad to see you, too. You had us worried there for a little bit."

"How did you figure it out?"

"Somebody saw you leaving with Melinda and Charlie thought it was weird," Ben said as he sawed through the ropes holding her hands in place.

"Well Charlie is right." Once he freed her hands, Jen rubbed her wrists and shrugged her shoulders trying to loosen up the stiffness.

"Damn, these ropes around your ankles are tight." He ran his hands over the rope binding her feet. The feel of his fingers tickled her skin. "I'm afraid I might end up cutting you."

"Don't worry. It's okay. I trust you," she said. Ben met her eyes. He gave her a nod and went back to work sawing the rope. Finally her feet were free and Ben pulled her to her feet as he stood up. She wobbled a little and pressed her hand to her forehead. "Whoa."

"You okay?" He put his hands on her shoulders to steady her.

"Yeah," she said. "I don't know what she did to me, but I can't shake this dizziness."

"Come, let's get you out of here." Ben took her hand and led her to the back door. When he touched it, the metal doorknob suddenly glowed red, burning his hand. Ben stifled a cry and yanked his hand back. Angry red skin striped his fingers and palm where he'd touched the knob. "Shit. She's booby-trapped the place."

"What?" Jen said, fighting the panic fluttering in her chest.

"Wait here." He dropped her hand and grabbed a kitchen towel from the towel bar on the end of the island. He wrapped the towel around his hand and punched through one of the panes of glass. As soon as he did, though, the glass pulled itself back together into a solid pane again. Ben took a step back from the door. "What the hell?"

"She must've put a binding spell on the house," Jen said.

"That's right. Very good," Melinda said, walking in through the kitchen doorway. "Hi there," she said in her perkiest voice. "I was wondering when we would see you again. I need you to do me the teensiest favor. You know that monitoring spell you put on my niece? Well I need you to break it."

Ben stepped in front of Jen and held up his scorched hand. "Melinda, let's just think this through for a minute. Okay? You're not going to get away with any of this. If you surrender now, I will make sure that the tribunal knows that you gave yourself up without causing any more bloodshed."

WENDY WANG

Melinda snickered, directing her question to Jen. "Is he serious?"

"He sounds serious to me," she said.

"Oh sugar, bless your heart," Melinda said. "That's not how things work in this house." In one fell swoop Melinda grabbed an iron frying pan from her stove top and slung it as hard and as fast as she could at Ben's head. His hands began to glow green, and he swiped at the pan. It crashed into the floor cracking and breaking the marble tile.

"Now look what you've done," Melinda growled. She pulled a knife from the block on the counter and threw it at him. Ben grabbed Jen's hand and pulled her as fast as he could into the butler's pantry off the kitchen leading to the formal dining room. He slammed the door behind them and locked it.

"You can't hide from me in this house," Melinda called after him.

Ben shoved the polished mahogany table against the door and started to pull Jen into the living room.

"Ben wait," Jen whispered. The world swirled in gray. "I'm not feeling so good."

Ben scooped her up into his arms and Jen rested her head in the crook of his neck, breathing him in. She didn't know how much longer she could stay conscious.

"Ben, she did something to me," she whispered and slipped into the darkness.

CHAPTER 20

Jason was the first to show up after Charlie sent a text for help. He rode into Melinda's subdivision with his blue lights flashing on the on the dash of his Dodge Charger. Charlie had parked down the street so as not to be conspicuous. As soon as she saw the lights she got out of her car and waved him down. Jason pulled up behind her and got out of his car.

"What's going on?" he said.

"I need your help. I think Melinda forced Jen into her car. And now she has her in her house. Ben went in about thirty minutes ago but I haven't seen or heard from him since."

"Maybe he and Melinda are just talking?" Jason said.

"I don't think so." Charlie pulled her phone from

her pocket and showed Jason the text from Ben. "That's why I texted you."

It simply read: I see Jen in the kitchen. Looks like she's tied to a chair. I'm going in.

"What the fuck?" Jason said.

"I know," Charlie said.

Jason reached into his car and grabbed his radio off the front seat.

"What are you doing? Charlie asked.

"I'm calling for backup," Jason said. "Holding somebody hostage just moved this into my territory."

"Can you wait?" Charlie asked." There's a spell on that house. I'm afraid that anybody who goes in may not be able to come out unless Melinda allows it."

Jason frowned and lowered his hand holding the radio. "Charlie, we need a hostage negotiator."

"It's not gonna work." Charlie shook her head. "Melinda is not thinking clearly. And quite honestly, I don't know what she's capable of. I know she can create a death spell, which makes her dangerous. I don't want you or anybody else to get hurt. You could go in and your guns could be rendered useless."

"Charlie," Jason said. "This is really a matter for the Sheriff's Department now. I'm sorry, but I'm going to have to override you on this." He squeezed the talk button on the side of the radio. "Dispatch this is

Sheriff Forty. I'm in Sector George. I need back up at a possible hostage situation. Suspect is a thirty-four-year-old female. Go ahead."

"Forty, I have two cars in the area, go ahead."

"Dispatch, contact Lieutenant Commander Beck and apprise him of the situation."

"Copy that Forty."

Jason let go of the button and clipped the radio to his waistband.

"Do you think she's armed?" Jason asked.

"Only with the spell book," Charlie said. "I don't know if your guns are going to work in there."

"What you mean?"

"There is a spell on that house. Its pulsing a dark energy unlike anything I've ever seen. I'm guessing it's some sort of binding spell."

"What does that mean? Binding spell?" Jason asked.

"It means that she may have put a spell on the house to keep people from either entering the house, leaving the house, or it could be a combination of both. Ultimately, she has the control," Charlie said.

"Okay, how do we get the control away from her?" Jason asked.

"Evangeline, Lisa and Daphne are on their way. We'll have to break the spell which I anticipate she's going to fight tooth and nail. I need y'all to run interference."

"Charlie," Jason said. "This is really a police matter now."

"Maybe I shouldn't have called you," Charlie said, pinching the bridge of her nose. "I didn't realize it was going to get so complicated."

Jason sighed and shook his head. "My goal is to get Jen out of there safely. I can give you some leeway but not a lot."

"All right," Charlie said, her voice emanating deep reluctance. "And we'll protect you and your men as best we can."

"Great," Jason said. His lips twisted into a grimace.

"What is it?" Charlie asked.

"I'm just trying to figure out how much shit Beck is gonna give me. He thinks all this is hoodoo."

Charlie scowled. "Hoodoo is a completely different set of skills."

"Well I'll be sure to let Beck know that." Jason rolled his eyes.

"Looks like the cavalry is here." Charlie pointed to Lisa's white BMW headed toward them. A pair of sheriff's cruisers followed close behind.

"Yes, they are," Jason said.

* * *

BECK'S UNMARKED CRUISER PARKED BEHIND JASON'S

Dodge Charger and the tall, lanky lieutenant commander hopped out.

"What the hell is this all about?" Beck said, taking a look at the two sheriff's cars parked directly in front of the house as cover. "We have a hostage situation? Why don't we have a negotiator out here yet?"

Charlie gave Jason an irritated look. Beck had a big mouth and big opinions to go with it.

"Hello, Lieutenant Beck," Evangeline said. Beck stopped short and his eyes widened at the sight of Charlie's aunt. He threw a what-the-hell look at Jason and put his hands on his slim hips.

Jason cleared his throat and said, "Charlie, you're with me." He gestured for Beck to follow them away from the cars for a little more privacy.

Beck glanced at the two deputies chatting with Evangeline and Daphne. "What the fuck? You have civilians on the scene?"

"Yes, I do. If you give me a minute I can explain," Jason said.

Beck's mouth twisted into a scowl. "I'm all ears."

"You know this pendant you were giving me a hard time about?" Jason said, pulling the pendant out of his shirt and showing it to Beck. "

"Yeah, so?" Beck said. "What does that have to do with the price of tea in China?"

"I gave it to him," Charlie said. "Actually my

cousin Jen gave it to him but Jason wears it for protection."

"I think your vest would be a better way to protect yourself," Beck scoffed.

"Lieutenant, I know this is going to be hard for you to swallow but there are dark forces in the world," Charlie said.

"No shit," Beck said. "I don't know where you're going with this—"

"Is everything all right over here?" Evangeline asked as she walked up and stood next to Charlie.

"No, ma'am it's not," Beck said. "No offense but I'm not sure what you're doing here."

"Oh," Evangeline said. "We've come to break the spell on that house so that you and your men can go in and safely get my niece out."

Beck furrowed his brow, his eyes flitting between Evangeline's serene expression and Jason's apprehensive face. Beck's voice overflowed with sarcasm as he spoke, "Oh, is that all?"

"Yeah, that's all," Jason said. "I don't know how else to say this, but there's a witch inside that house and she's gonna use magic against us if we try to go in there before Charlie and her family break the spell on the house."

"Have you lost your damn mind?" Beck asked.

"No," Jason said. "Magic is real. Charlie and her family are witches."

"Yeah? Can you fly on a broom?" Beck said half-teasing.

"I can't," Charlie said. "But Evangeline's been known to on occasion."

"Y'all are crazy," Beck said and pointed at Jason. "And you're the craziest for buying into this shit."

"Maybe I am, but I've seen what they can do," Jason said.

Evangeline reached out and gently touched Beck on the top of his arm. "I really appreciate you being here, Lieutenant Beck. Your assistance in this matter is vital."

Beck's face slackened and the lines in his forehead smoothed. "Thank you ma'am," he said in a dreamy voice. "We're here to serve and protect."

I know you are Lieutenant," Evangeline said. "Now if you boys wouldn't mind, we need to get to work."

"Yes ma'am," Beck said.

"Once we break the spell we need you to go up to the door and ring the bell," Evangeline said.

"I rang it earlier," Charlie said. "That's when I felt the spell really lock into place."

"We'll do whatever it takes ma'am," Beck said.

"Thank you," Evangeline said. "Now why don't you go over and chat with your friends by the sheriff's cars."

"Yes ma'am," Beck said.

Charlie waited until Beck was out of hearing range before turning to her aunt. "What did you just do?"

"Desperate times call for desperate measures," Evangeline said. "I just used a little suggestibility spell, that's all."

"Have you ever done that to me?" Jason asked.

"No, of course not," Charlie said. "Not that I haven't about thought about it."

Jason scowled. "All right. We've got their compliance."

"Let's form the circle. And go get our girl," Evangeline said.

CHAPTER 21

Jen jerked her head up and blinked her eyes, taking in her surroundings. She was sitting on the floor next to a painted gold accent table.

Then she remembered Melinda and Ben. She had passed out. She struggled against the ropes binding her arms to her body but it was more than that. She felt something warm pressing against her back. She tried to turn her head so she could look behind her but found it almost impossible.

"Good," Ben said. "You're awake. "How are you feeling?"

"Like a freight train ran through my head," Jen said. "What happened?"

"When you passed out, she was able to trip me. I dropped you I'm afraid, and she kicked me in the head before I could react. When I woke up, I was bound to you."

"What are we going to do?" Jen asked.

"I'm not quite sure. There's a binding spell on this house."

"Yeah, I remember that part," Jen said.

"The one thing we have going for us is that Charlie's outside," Ben said.

"By herself?"

"Hopefully not," Ben said. "We agreed on a signal and if she didn't hear from me she was supposed to call for backup."

"Okay," Jen said. "That's good. That means my family is probably on the way if they're not already here. So we just need to sit tight."

"Right," Ben said. "Or—"

"Or?" Jen said.

"Or we can try to get out of here ourselves," Ben said. "Just in case."

"How do you propose we do that?"

"Look," Ben said softly.

"In case you hadn't noticed I can't turn around," Jen snapped.

"Right, sorry," Ben said. "Layla keeps peeking in here. I don't think she expected her aunt to take hostages."

"I don't think anybody expected her to take hostages," Jen said.

"Well, rejection can sometimes hit people hard," Ben said.

"What is that supposed to mean?" Jen said.

"Nothing. I mean if you look at what happened to her, she couldn't control her husband anymore, and he left her for another woman. Obviously that's pushed her over the edge."

"Right," Jen said.

"What did you think I was talking about?"

"I don't know. Nothing." Jen wiggled against the ropes.

"Okay." Ben's voice was full of doubt.

Jen sighed. "I just thought—"

"Layla," Ben said. "I can see you. Please Layla. I know that you think this is not right."

Jen tried to turn her head but she still couldn't see anything. Since she and Ben were tied back to back, he blocked most of her view.

"I shouldn't be talking to you," Layla whispered harshly. "And if you know what's good for you," Layla paused to look over her shoulder, "you will just do whatever my aunt wants to do."

Ben whispered, "I know you're scared of her. I saw it on your face earlier. If you help us get out of here, I think I have a solution for you."

Jen heard the girl move closer. "What kind of solution?"

"I was a lot like you when I was growing up.

Rebellious, always getting in trouble. And that was compounded by the fact that I could do magic. I ended up getting a warning from the DOL, too."

"You did?" Layla said.

"Yep. It turned out the to be the best thing that ever happened to me. The DOL has a program specifically for mentoring young witches. With your situation I can help you get into it."

"Layla!" Melinda yelled from another room. "Come here."

"I — I have to go," Layla said. She jumped up and fled the room. Ben let out a deep sigh.

"Dammit," he said.

"Give her time to think about that," Jen said. "It's a scary and overwhelming offer for somebody to help you. When you're in a bad situation."

"Sounds like you have some experience with that," Ben said.

"Maybe," Jen said. "Was that story you told her about you true?"

"Every word." Ben said. "Maybe if we get out of here, I'll tell you about it sometime."

Jens lips curved up. "If we get out of here, I think I would very much like to hear that story."

"Good. I'd like to hear your story, too," Ben said.

The house shook and for a moment Jen thought it might be an earthquake. She had experienced them firsthand when she lived in California but they were only the stuff of legends on the coast of South Carolina. A huge earthquake had hit the city of Charleston over a hundred and thirty years ago. Dust from the ceiling rained down on them and a large crack formed over the mantle of the fireplace.

"Ben," Jen said, trying to keep her voice from sounding hysterical. "What's happening?"

"I don't know," he said.

The large crystal chandelier shook overhead. "Ben, look up. We have got to move."

"Shit," he muttered.

A moment later, Layla dashed in with a knife in her hand. "We don't have much time." The sound of a little girl screaming and then crying came from above their heads. "My aunt is upstairs with Camille."

She sliced through the rope freeing them both. Jen pushed out against the cut sisal and it dropped to the floor. Ben got up leaving her back cold. He reached down and took her hand pulling her to her feet.

"Come on," Layla said. "Your friend is outside. They're in a circle holding hands and chanting from what I can tell."

"They're trying to break the spell," Jen and Ben said at the same time.

"Come on!" Layla said, walking backwards. Ben took Jen's hand, and they began to follow Layla through the house toward the back door. Drywall from the ceiling crashed down and large plumes of dust filled the air. Layla led them through the dining room and Butler's pantry into the kitchen. The glass from the French door exploded, covering them in glass. The brass door handle glowed red and Jen didn't dare touch it.

"Layla!" Melinda screamed from the kitchen door. Melinda carried her terrified daughter as the world crashed around them.

Ben grabbed hold of Jen and held onto her, shielding her head with his body.

"Aunt Melinda, break the spell," Layla pleaded.

"She's right, Melinda. Break the spell," Ben said. "If you break it this will all be over."

"No, it won't," Melinda said. "Not after what I've done."

"We'll find a way, Melinda. Break the spell, let us out. If not for us, for your daughter," Jen said.

Something shifted in Melinda's face. "Layla, take Camille."

Layla took the girl from her aunt despite the child's protests.

"Go, go with Layla, baby." Melinda stroked her daughter's hair. "It's going to be okay. I'm gonna make it stop now."

Camille wrapped her arms around Layla's neck and they hugged each other tight. Melinda disappeared through the kitchen door.

"Come on," Ben said. He picked up one of the kitchen chairs and threw it through the grill of wood. He pushed Jen through first and then Layla and Camille. The four of them rushed into the yard. The building gave one loud groan, a thunderous rumble as the first floor imploded, sending dust and debris out in every direction.

"Oh sweet goddess," Jen said as realization washed over her. "Melinda was still in there." Ben put a hand on her shoulder and she turned, pressing her face against his chest. He wrapped his arms around her.

"I don't think she ever meant to come out," Ben said softly against the top of her head. Jen hugged him tighter.

"We need to let them know that we're safe," Jen said. Ben stroked her hair and held her for a moment longer before they went to find her family.

CHAPTER 22

"What's going to happen to Camille?" Charlie sat on the back-porch swing of her uncle Jack's house. She pulled her knees to her chest and rested her chin on top of them.

"She's gonna go live with her dad." Jen sat in one of the old metal chairs and rocked back and forth.

"And they never found Melinda's body?" Lisa sat next to Charlie on the porch swing.

"According to Jason they didn't find any human remains in the rubble," Charlie said.

"You think she escaped?" Jen asked.

"I don't know," Charlie said. "That whole thing is just very strange. I mean once the building started to shake, we stopped the ritual to break the spell."

"Right, but the building still shook." Daphne

leaned back in the chair across from Charlie and Lisa. She took a sip of the mimosa that Jen had made.

"Ben thinks she may have just continued to bring the house down as a way to escape," Jen said.

"Is he going to go after her?" Lisa asked.

"I don't think so." Jen said.

"What's going to happen to Layla?" Charlie asked.

"There's an apprenticeship program for witches like Layla that have no family and need someone to give them some guidance," Jen said.

"I don't know about that," Lisa said. "That whole program makes me nervous."

"Why?" Jen asked.

Lisa frowned. "Because entities like the DOL? They don't do anything altruistic. Oh, they may say it's for the greater good but more than likely they are investing all that training into kids like Layla so that they have their own little army of mercenaries that can carry out their laws and judgments."

Charlie shook her head. "That may not be such a bad thing. She'll get to learn how to really control her magic and make some friends who are like her," Charlie said. "It may be a mixed bag I don't think you have to be so cynical about it."

"Well, maybe," Lisa said.

Charlie glanced at her cousin. "You know, I'm

sorry I got mad at you Lisa. If you and Jason want date, I think that's great."

"We're not dating. Not exactly," Lisa protested, but her lips curved into a smile as she said it.

"Right," Daphne said. "It's just a little slutty fun, right?"

"I am not a slut!" Lisa sat up straight, a look of disgust wrinkling her forehead.

"Nobody thinks you're a slut," Jen said.

Daphne cocked her head. "Well some people think she's a slut."

"Daphne! Hush." Jen scolded.

"What?" Daphne grumbled. "It's pretty common knowledge that she slept with her partner."

"I did not sleep with any of my partners. God!" Lisa banged her hand down on the arms of the swing, making it shake.

"Well that's what people say," Daphne said in a small voice. "They say that you slept with one of the partners to make partner."

"Are you freaking kidding me?" Lisa snapped. "I made partner because I worked my ass off for eight and a half years. You would think the people in this town had better things to talk about than me and my career! Oh and thanks for partaking in the sexism, Daphne. That's just great."

"I don't think you're slutty," Daphne protested.

"I'm just telling you what people say. I hear a lot in my work."

"Well people suck! And you suck too for not standing up for me," Lisa said, sounding wounded.

Daphne frowned. "You're right. I'm sorry. Sometimes it's just easier to nod my head and keep quiet. I'm sorry, really."

"I just wish I understood why," Lisa said.

"I can tell you that," Charlie said softly. Lisa shifted her gaze to her cousin. "It's the same reason I was mad at you. Which I guess means I suck too. You're smart and you're beautiful and you are tough as nails and driven as hell. You stand up and get what you want and that includes men. And when you do, they fall for you, Lisa. Hard. Every single one of them. I guess I was just scared that Jason might fall for you, too."

"Were you jealous?" Jen asked.

"Maybe a little." Charlie shrugged. "But not because I wanted to date Jason. I don't. I swear on the stars above. It's just ... the whole reason any of y'all even know him is because of me. It's silly." Charlie shook her head and rolled her eyes at herself. "But it was more than that, too."

"You're afraid I will hurt him," Lisa said.

"You don't exactly have a great track record," Charlie said. "I don't think you mean to hurt the guys, I really don't. I think that because you're so great and because these men fall hard for you it scares the crap out of you. And you turn tail and run every single time. The problem that comes in is before you take off, you turn around and crush them with your boot heel to make sure they don't follow you."

Lisa's green eyes widened, becoming glassy and her lips quivered.

"Oh honey, I didn't mean to make you cry."

"I'm not crying." Lisa muttered under her breath. She turned her head and wiped at the corners of her eyes.

Charlie wrapped her arm around Lisa's shoulder. "You know it would be okay if you were. I won't tell anybody that you're actually human. Cross my heart."

Lisa rested her head on Charlie's shoulder. "I don't want you to worry. Jason and I agreed that we would be together as long as it was fun. That's all. It's not going to get serious. Neither one of us has time for that. And you know he's not the only one that could get hurt. Jason's pretty great, too." Lisa wrapped her arm around Charlie's waist, and Charlie hugged her tighter, comforting her.

"I know," Charlie said.

"You like him," Jen said, only half teasing.

"What's not to like? Have you seen his chest?" Lisa said.

Jen made a singing noise in the back of her throat, grinning. "You do like him. And not for his chest. And no, I have not, thank you very much."

"Well just know that if you chase Jason off he's not going to come back like Billy did," Charlie said.

"Yeah, you know, I never could figure that out," Daphne said. "Billy just kept coming back, and you just let him wheedle his way back in."

"Bless his heart. It's not Billy's fault that he's dumb as a post," Jen said.

"Hush up. Billy was always sweet to me and he made me laugh. I just didn't see spending my life with him that's all."

"Well there's definitely something to be said for a sweet, funny man," Charlie said.

"Amen to that," Jen and Daphne said in a chorus.

"So are we all good?" Charlie asked squeezing Lisa's shoulders a little tighter.

"Yeah," Lisa said nodding.

"Yeah," Jen said.

"Yeah," Daphne said.

"Good," Charlie said. "Now I don't know about y'all but I've been thinking about the salted caramel pie in the icebox all afternoon."

"Come on," Jen said. "I'll slice it up. Daphne would you please get the dessert dishes out of the cupboard?"

"Sure." Daphne grinned and hopped up from her chair.

"I'll get the silver," Charlie said.

Lisa sniffed and straightened up. "And I'll get the pitcher of mimosas."

The End

AUTHOR'S NOTE

Thank you for reading. If you loved this book and want the adventure, you can download the next book in the series The Harbinger.

If you love Charlie and want to go along on her ghostly adventures, please join my readers list: http://eepurl.com/czMPg1

By signing up you'll get a free deleted scene from this book and you'll be the first to know about major updates and new releases.

If you enjoyed this book, please give it a rating on Amazon. Your kind words and encouragement can make an author's day (ask me how I know – smile). Of course, I'll keep writing whether you give me an Outstanding review or not, but it might get done faster with your cheerleading (smile).

Want to comment on your favorite scene? Or

make suggestions for a funny ghostly encounter for Charlie? Or tell me what sort of magic you'd like to see Jen, Daphne and Lisa perform? Or take part in naming the killers/ghosts for my future books? Come tell me on Facebook.

Facebook: **https://www.facebook.com/wendy-wangauthor** or let's talk about our favorite books in my readers group on Facebook;

Readers **Group**: **https://www.facebook.com/groups/128734862802294 0/**;

or you can always drop me an email,

Email: **http://www.wendywangbooks.com/contact.html**

Thank you again for reading!

Check out my other books:

Witches of Palmetto Point Series (Supernatural Suspense)
Book 1: Haunting Charlie
Book 2: Wayward Spirits
Book 3: Devil's Snare
Book 4: The Witch's Ladder

The Book of Kaels Series (Fantasy)
Book 1: The Last Queen

Book 2: The Wood Kael
Book 3: The Metal Kael
Book 4: The Fire Kael
Book of Kaels Box Set: Books 1 -4
Short Stories: Love Lacey

<<<<>>>

Made in the USA
Middletown, DE
27 June 2024

56400711R00167